Books by Steven Butler

THE WRONG PONG
HOLIDAY HULLABALOO

THE WRONG PONG
HOLIDAY HULLABALOO

STEVEN BUTLER

Illustrated by Chris Fisher

PUFFIN

For Shirley, Ron, Jenny, David and Ava . . .
A potato family of great jubbliness

PUFFIN BOOKS

Published by the Penguin Group
Penguin Books Ltd, 80 Strand, London WC2R 0RL, England
Penguin Group (USA) Inc., 375 Hudson Street, New York, New York 10014, USA
Penguin Group (Canada), 90 Eglinton Avenue East, Suite 700, Toronto, Ontario, Canada M4P 2Y3
(a division of Pearson Penguin Canada Inc.)
Penguin Ireland, 25 St Stephen's Green, Dublin 2, Ireland (a division of Penguin Books Ltd)
Penguin Group (Australia), 250 Camberwell Road, Camberwell, Victoria 3124, Australia
(a division of Pearson Australia Group Pty Ltd)
Penguin Books India Pvt Ltd, 11 Community Centre, Panchsheel Park, New Delhi – 110 017, India
Penguin Group (NZ), 67 Apollo Drive, Rosedale, Auckland, 0632, New Zealand
(a division of Pearson New Zealand Ltd)
Penguin Books (South Africa) (Pty) Ltd, 24 Sturdee Avenue, Rosebank, Johannesburg 2196, South Africa

Penguin Books Ltd, Registered Offices: 80 Strand, London WC2R 0RL, England

puffinbooks.com

First published 2011

006

Set in 13/20pt Baskerville MT Std
Printed in Great Britain by Clays Ltd, St Ives plc

British Library Cataloguing in Publication Data
A CIP catalogue record for this book is available from the British Library

ISBN: 978–0–141–33391–5

www.greenpenguin.co.uk

Contents

A Note

Neville stared, wide-eyed, into the toilet bowl. His mouth twitched into a smile and the hairs on the back of his neck stood on end.

There floating on the surface of the water was a single square of toilet tissue. On it in scruffy handwriting were the words:

Unwelcome Guests

Neville peeked through the crack in the kitchen door. It was lunchtime as normal in the Brisket house. Marjorie stood baking with a pink, sparkly apron and matching rubber gloves. She was singing to herself in her shrill voice like a parrot with a cold.

'Erm, Mum?' Neville said, edging into the kitchen. His mum was going to go crazy. She turned and glared at him.

'What?' Marjorie snapped. 'I'm cooking.'

'I got a letter,' Neville said. 'I . . . erm . . .'

'Neville Brisket, what are you talking about? I'm trying to get ahead with supper. Can't you see my soufflé needs me right now?'

'I think . . . erm . . . I think you should read it.' Neville held out the piece of toilet tissue and waited for Marjorie to explode. *The Bulches, here?* he thought.

A family of galumphing, toadstool-covered trolls were coming to stay. Neville was excited at the thought of seeing his other family from down the toilet, but even he couldn't imagine what would happen if they were let loose in Victoria Avenue. Neville started inching away as his mum read the note.

'AAAAAAAAGGGGHHH!' Marjorie dropped her freshly baked bean-sprout soufflé on to the kitchen floor. It landed with a sticky *SLAP* and splattered all over Neville's slippers.

'WWWWWHHHHHAAAATTTT?' she screamed. 'THEY CAN'T!' Marjorie started running on the spot and flapping her arms like a demented rooster. 'THOSE THINGS? THOSE THINGS IN *MY* HOUSE?'

'But they're family now, remember?' Neville said, shrinking away from his flailing mother. He wasn't feeling very brave for an honorary troll.

'No, I don't remember,' Marjorie shouted back. 'Do you know what is happening today? *DO YOU?*'

Neville opened his mouth to answer, but his mum wasn't listening.

'Today is the most dreadful day in the history of the world,' she said, fanning herself and looking dramatically at the ceiling. 'This evening your rich grandma Joan is coming to stay. Do you know how bad that is? That vicious old weasel is horrible enough to us, and we're her family. She'll scream the house down if she sees trolls here. She'll call the police, and probably the fire brigade as well. All the neighbours will know our secret and no one will speak to us ever again!'

Marjorie looked like she was going to take off like a rocket. She actually might have done if Herbert hadn't walked in through the back door with Napoleon the dog trotting behind him like a poo on a lead.

'Oh dear,' he said, seeing Marjorie's face. 'Anything the matter?'

'AAAAAAGGGHHH!' Marjorie threw the toilet tissue at Herbert, dived into the living room and snatched up a cushion from the sofa.

'The Bulches are coming to stay,' Neville told his dad.

'What? Them . . . them troll things? Staying here at the same time as your grandmother?' Herbert's face turned pale. 'Your mum's not going to like that.'

'No,' said Neville.

In the living room, Marjorie screamed again.

'Maybe one of my whale music CDs would help?' said Herbert, peeking round the living-room door at Marjorie rocking back and forth on the carpet.

Either that or a bucket of cold water poured over her head, thought Neville.

'Trolls,' Marjorie blubbed. 'NAIL DOWN THE TOILET SEATS!'

'Steady on, love,' said Herbert.

'BRICK UP THE DOORFRAMES!'

'They won't be any trouble,' Neville said from the doorway. 'Honest.' He thought he'd better not fetch the bucket just yet.

'Trouble? They're thieving, stinking, filthy trolls – they're made of trouble!'

Neville shuffled a little bit closer to his mother. 'I promise I'll hide them up in my room when Grandma Joan arrives,' he said. Deep down inside, Neville secretly wished the Bulches would frighten the nasty old bat away forever. 'She'll never notice them.'

'What about that little one – Plop? He's bound to wreck my home.'

'His name's Pong,' said Neville.

'Pong, Plop, what does it matter? WE'RE DOOMED!'

'I'll keep an extra eye on him,' Neville said. 'I promise nothing bad will happen.'

'You'd better hope you're right, Neville Brisket,' Marjorie hissed, pointing a skinny pink rubber finger at him. 'If those monsters rear their ugly heads while Joan is about, she'll make curtains out

of them. How would you like that? Waking up each morning to a lovely set of troll-skin curtains?'

Neville had butterflies in his stomach. The more he looked at his mum, the more she reminded him of a slurch – a wailing gnashing monster from the land of the trolls, complete with teeth like screwdrivers.

'You'd better keep them out of my sight, Neville Brisket,' snarled Marjorie.

'I promise,' he said with a gulp.

The Family Bulch

Neville had that same feeling in his belly that he always got on Christmas Eve. The waiting was unbearable. It was almost dinnertime and they still hadn't arrived.

He sat biting his fingernails, while Marjorie shivered next to him and Herbert paced back and forth across the living-room rug. He looked like a polar bear at the zoo, thought Neville, only less cuddly.

The only noise in the whole house was the scuffing of Herbert's feet and the ticking of the hallway clock.

Just when Neville was starting to think the Bulches weren't coming after all, he heard the distant knock of the upstairs toilet lid being lifted. Followed by the *SPLOSH-STOMP . . . SPLOSH-STOMP* of large wet feet stepping on to the tiles.

'They're here,' Marjorie wailed, hiding her face behind her hands. 'Trolls in my house . . . AGAIN!'

Neville got up from the sofa, his heart pounding against his ribs. He suddenly felt very nervous. It had been so long since he'd seen his mooma and dooda. What if they weren't as friendly as he remembered? What if they'd come to take him away again?

THUD . . . THUD . . . THUD . . .

Neville listened to the clomp of troll feet coming down the stairs. The living-room door handle jiggled. Everyone held their breath.

'How d'you work this thing?' came a voice on the other side. It was Clod's voice. 'It's broken.'

'Like this, you nogginknocker,' came Malaria's voice. The handle jiggled again, but nothing happened. 'Well, I never.'

The handle jiggled one last time, followed by a dull clunk. It sounded as though it had fallen off altogether.

'Oh well . . . Not to worry,' said Clod. Then there was silence.

'I think they're going home,' whispered Herbert. 'Listen – nothing.'

Marjorie's face was just beginning to crease into a smile when Malaria burst through the living-room wall to the side of the door. 'See, Clod,' she said, chuckling. 'That's how it works.'

She stomped through in a cloud of dust and cement and broken brick. Clod lumbered through after her.

Neville's heart was racing faster and faster. There they were. His mooma and dooda, his troll parents, back from Underneath.

There was a strange moment of silence when the Bulches and the Briskets just stared at each other. Clod and Malaria had come dressed for the occasion in their finest clothes. Clod was wearing his ten-sizes-too-small trollabaloo suit and Malaria wore a lacy gown that looked like it had been made from three wedding dresses all stitched together, and an enormous hat of woven swamp grass.

'NEV!' Clod rushed forward and scooped Neville up in a bulky troll hug. ''Ello, lump,' he said,

beaming. 'What a sight for salty eyes you are.'

Now they'd arrived, Neville was so pleased to see the trolls that for a second he thought he was going to cry. He thought his parents might too, but for a very different reason. Herbert had picked up a piece of the wall and was gawping at it. Marjorie's face was now the colour of tomato ketchup and her mouth was saying lots of rude words, but no sound was coming out.

'BBRRRROOOOOAAAAAAGGGGHH!' Pong bounded through the hole in the wall and leapt into Marjorie's arms. He licked her face like an excited puppy.

'Get off! GET OFF!' Marjorie screamed.

'Now, Pong,' said Malaria. 'Say hello nicely to . . . to . . . Hergberg and Margarine?'

'Herbert and Marjorie,' said Marjorie sharply, but Malaria wasn't listening. Marjorie dropped Pong and he skittered off to the kitchen. In no time, the sound of teacups smashing and Pong cooing with glee came back through the open doorway.

'I'd forgotten how honksome you are, my porklet,' Malaria said, flinging her arms round both Clod and Neville. 'Did you miss your mooma?'

'Of course,' shouted Neville. 'We're so glad you're here, aren't we, Mum and Dad!'

Herbert looked at Marjorie, who squeaked, wobbled, then fainted. No one except Napoleon noticed. He padded across the living room and curled up on top of Marjorie's warm belly.

'I thought you might be,' laughed Clod, lifting Neville away from him to get a good look. 'It's been blunkin' ages since we had a nice trolliday.'

'I wanted to go for a winky little break in the fungus forests,' said Malaria. 'But then Rubella said we should glump off to see you overlings.'

Neville stiffened in Clod's grip.

'Rubella's here too?' he said, breaking out in a cold sweat.

'Of course!' Clod chuckled. 'It was her idea.' He put Neville down gently on the cement-covered rug and turned to the hole in the living-room wall. 'Belly, get your face out of that laundry basket and come and see your brother. There'll be humpfuls of time for food later.'

'She's as greedy as a gundiskump,' said Malaria.

THUD . . . THUD . . . THUD . . . THUD . . . THUD . . .

Rubella stomped down the stairs. Then, like a bad dream emerging through the last wisps of dust, she appeared, scowling as usual. Neville gasped. He clapped his hands over his mouth and was very nearly sick. Rubella was wearing a . . . a . . . A BIKINI!!!!

Her massive, greasy belly hung over the yellow bikini bottoms like a sack of boiled chickens and the bikini top was way too small. She was bulging out in all directions like an over-inflated balloon.

Rubella tossed her spiny hair over her turnip shoulders, stuck her hands on her boulder-sized hips and glared.

'All right, scab?' she hissed, like a bullock with a bad case of warts. 'Bleeucchh, you're ugly.'

Meanwhile

Joan Brisket clattered along the dark hallway of her enormous mansion house, muttering to herself. She was in a foul mood. The thought of having to spend a whole day with her idiot son, his common-as-muck wife and their insect of a child made her feel positively sick. Neville? Who would call their child Neville?

She squinted at the mirror and painted a thick layer of pink lipstick on to her puckered-up lips. They were like a pair of slugs that had shrivelled and gone wrinkly in the sun.

A servant carrying a tray of glasses passed her as she headed for the front door. Joan stuck her walking stick out and tripped him up. He fell to the ground with an almighty *SMASH*.

'NO WAGES FOR A MONTH!' Joan yelled, then chuckled quietly to herself.

She stopped at the hat rack and snatched up a fox-fur scarf. She'd shot and skinned the fox with her own hands and it was her favourite. Then she rang a small bell to call for her driver and, stepping out into the cold air, set off to visit her awful relatives.

Trolliday Trouble

Neville clenched his bottom and gripped his toes to stop himself from running out of the room.

'I said . . . All right, scab?' Rubella asked again.

'Hello,' squeaked Neville. He was determined not to look scared and wimpy in front of his hulking great walrus of a troll-sister, but it wasn't easy. Neville thought of Captain Brilliant to make himself feel braver. 'It's nice to see you, Rubella,' Neville lied. 'You look . . . erm . . .'

Rubella clicked her tongue and rolled her eyes.

'You look like a right beachy beauty,' Clod said to his daughter with an even bigger grin. Neville nodded and pulled his best 'I agree' face.

'It's a good thing you found that book, Belly,' Malaria said. 'This was a squibbly idea.'

'What book?' Neville asked.

'This,' said Rubella, pulling a rolled-up magazine

out of her bikini bottoms. She held it up for Neville to see.

'That's mine,' said Herbert suddenly, stepping over Marjorie, who was still out cold. It was one of his old *Happy Holiday* magazines (the kind that tells you where to go and what to see). 'I threw that out last week when Napoleon peed on it.'

'Well, it's mine now,' Rubella snapped. She opened the tattered front page. 'And it says here: "When you arrive at your holiday destination you can expect to be pampered with exotic drinks and fancy nibbles."'

'Yes . . . b-but . . .' Herbert stammered.

'We've arrived at our trolliday destination.'

Herbert's bottom lip started to tremble.

'I WANT MY FANCY NIBBLES!' Rubella roared. 'NOW!'

Herbert was almost knocked off his feet by the great gust of sour-smelling breath. He squealed like a mouse and ran out of the room.

'And,' Rubella said, turning to Neville, 'it says: "While on holiday you can enjoy lovely luxuries like foot massages, swimming, bathing, sports and entertainment."'

'How exciterous!' chuckled Malaria. 'Can you imagine? ME . . . BATHING? I've never had a bath in my life.'

Rubella plonked herself down on the sofa, lifted a spade-sized foot and rested it on top of Marjorie as if she was a stool. 'I'll have that foot massage now, Nev,' she said, wiggling her chubby toes and smiling a vinegary smile.

Neville ran for the door.

Five minutes later, Neville was equipped with gardening gloves, a tea towel tied over his nose and mouth and a pair of Herbert's skiing goggles. If he had to touch Rubella's revolting, clammy feet, he was going to do it safely.

He stopped at the living-room door and gawped in shock at the scene before him. How had this happened?

Furniture was upturned in all directions, there

were cushions scattered over the floor and the trolls were settling in for their holiday.

Herbert was standing like a waiter, holding a tray of left socks and old, mealy teabags for Rubella as he sobbed to himself.

'It says you're supposed to be entertaining me,' Rubella shouted at him, as she read the magazine. Every time she shouted, her belly wobbled like the world's largest jelly. 'Sing, slave . . . SING.'

Clod had found Herbert's golf clubs and, with a huge grin on his face, was launching golf balls around the room like little missiles. 'I feel like a right regular overling,' he said, chuckling.

Pong bounded back and forth through the hole in the wall as he chased Napoleon. The little dog had an upside-down teapot on his head and Neville could hear excited *yip-yips* coming from the downward-pointing spout.

Marjorie was still out cold, but was now slumped in one of the dining chairs with a wild hairdo of pigtails and spikes, all held together with rubber bands from the bureau drawer. Both her socks were missing and her toenails had been sloppily painted pink. The tin of pink paint lay on its side next to a paintbrush from the shed, spilling across the carpet.

Neville's heart raced. What was he going to do? At this rate there wouldn't be a house left for much longer. The thought of Grandma Joan seeing this made his blood run cold.

On the far side of the room, the garden doors were wide open and Neville could see Malaria hunkering down by the flowerbeds and rubbing handfuls of mud on to her face.

Neville gasped. This was worse than he thought. What would the neighbours say if they looked out of the window and saw a troll in the Briskets' daffodils?

'Squibbly. This'll do wonders for my warts,' Malaria mumbled. She'd practically dug up the entire garden and looked like a mud monster.

'This is the life,' she sighed. Then she twisted to look back through the garden doors. 'Margarine!' she shouted to Marjorie. 'D'you fancy a mudmask? It's good for your jowels . . . Margarine? *MARGARINE!*'

Neville had to do something. Joan would be arriving soon and it was up to him to get everything under control. He tore the tea towel away from his face, planted his feet wide apart – just like Captain Brilliant does – and yelled 'STTOOOOOOOOOPP!' as loudly as he could.

Everybody stopped what they were doing and goggled at Neville. Rubella spat out the left sock she was chewing on, while Herbert made a quick dash through the kitchen door to escape and shut himself in the cupboard under the sink. Clod let go of his golf club in mid-swing and it flew across the room and smashed the window. 'Oooops,' he mumbled. Pong came back through the hole in the wall and Malaria stomped in from the garden, dripping squidgy mud everywhere and forming a little brown moat round her on the carpet.

'What's wrong with YOU?' Rubella barked at Neville.

'*Look at this mess!*' he said.

The Bulches looked around the room.

'What mess?'

'My mum will go bananas when she wakes up and sees this!' said Neville.

'Oh, my little grunty-groaner,' Malaria said, plodding over and putting a wet arm round Neville's shoulders. 'Stop your worrying, my lump. Margarine's havin' a jubbly ole time. Look.' Malaria gave Marjorie a shake.

'What the –?' Marjorie muttered, slowly opening her eyes.

''Ello, Margarine,' Clod said, waving.

'I was just sayin', weren't I, Nev?' said Malaria. 'That you're havin' a bumfy old time, aren't you?'

Marjorie glanced at Malaria and then down at her feet. She wriggled her pink-painted toes with a look of fright. Then she touched her new hairdo.

'Huh?' said Marjorie.

'You look squibbly,' Malaria added. 'I did it myself.'

'I can see that,' said Rubella. 'Margarine, you look like a right daft donker.'

Marjorie turned and scowled at Rubella.

'Don't she, Dooda?' Rubella continued. 'Don't she look like mittens dressed as marmalade?'

Neville watched with butterflies in his belly as his mother turned round, saw all the mess and started dribbling with rage.

'ENOUGH!' Marjorie squawked. She launched herself at the nearest troll she saw, which happened to be Clod. Grabbing him by the lapels of his ten-sizes-too-small suit jacket, she pulled herself up to his eye line, pressed her nose against the end of his and screamed as loudly as shc could. Neville had never seen his mother so angry.

'YOU CAN SNATCH MY SON DOWN THE LOO! YOU CAN CHASE MY DOG AND STEAL ALL THE LEFT SOCKS! BUT DON'T YOU EVER, EVER, EVER MAKE A MESS IN MY HOME!'

Malaria and Rubella looked completely shocked. Clod's lower lip started to tremble.

'NOW YOU'RE GOING TO SIT DOWN AT THE TABLE LIKE REGULAR PEOPLE,' Marjorie ordered, '*AND SHUT UP!*'

Fancy Nibbles

'Well, I'll be a munkle's mumble,' said Clod, poking at the plate in front of him. He shrugged at Neville, who was sitting on the other side of the table. 'I ain't never seen nothin' like it.'

'What is it?' asked Rubella, stabbing at the white glop with a knife.

'I think it's slug purée,' said Malaria, rubbing her hands together and licking her lips. 'Good thing too . . . I'm starvatious.'

'That,' hissed Marjorie, with all the venom of a cobra with a headache, 'is your dinner. It's bean-sprout soufflé.'

'Bean sprout?' said Malaria, looking disappointed.

'A *WHAT*-flay?' sneered Rubella.

'SOUFFLÉ!' shouted Marjorie. 'NOW SIT QUIETLY AND EAT THIS . . . AND IF I SEE ANY OF YOU MOVE SO MUCH AS

AN INCH FROM YOUR CHAIR, I'LL . . . I'LL . . .' Marjorie picked up a spare fork from the table and flung it at the door. It stuck in the wood with a high-pitched *twang-ang-ang*. 'DO YOU UNDERSTAND?'

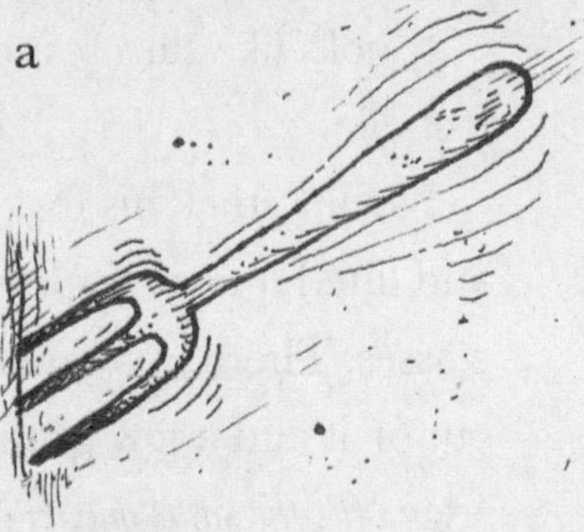

Everyone nodded silently.

'GOOD!'

Then Marjorie stormed off into the kitchen to try and coax Herbert out from the cupboard under the sink.

'D'you think she might be a bit moodsie?' whispered Malaria behind her hand. 'Must be something Hergberg said.'

Neville looked down at the lumpy white glop in front of him . . . bean-sprout soufflé? Was it the same bean-sprout soufflé that had been in a heap on the kitchen floor earlier that day? Whatever it was, the Bulches were all sitting up at the table and not causing any trouble. Neville breathed a small sigh of relief.

'I'm all giddy and nervish,' said Clod. He picked his plate up and gave it a big troll-sized sniff. 'My first try of overling food.'

'Looks like slurch snot, if you ask me,' said Rubella.

Neville stuck his fork in a big chunk of soufflé and lifted it near his face. He squinted through his glasses. There was one of Napoleon's hairs sticking out of it and a few grains of dirt clinging to the edge. *It's the same one,* he thought. *Mum has actually scooped it up from the kitchen floor and served it for dinner.*

'Ewwww,' said Neville and pushed his plate away.

'You can't do that,' said Clod.

'Margarine's gone to a lot of trouble preparing this . . . erm –' Malaria didn't look too sure –

'tummytinkling treat.'

'But there are dog hairs in it,' said Neville. 'And dirt from the kitchen floor.'

Clod's face brightened.

'Mmmmmm,' said Rubella, hooking up a long piece with her finger.

'Thank my lucky bits,' sighed Malaria, spooning a big glob of the stuff into Pong's open mouth. 'I was so worried. It looked 'orrible.'

The Bulches were soon tucking into their hair-riddled soufflé like greedy pigs round a trough, licking and gobbling great chunks of it without even using their knife and fork.

'Whoever knew that overlings could cook?' said Clod between mouthfuls. 'This on its own would be rotsome, but the dog hair gives it a lovely zingy tang.'

'This is what trollidays are all about,' said Malaria. 'Jubbly.'

Rubella finished first. She guzzled down the last scrap of her dinner and smashed the plate on the floor next to her.

'FINISHED!' she yelled.

'Sshhhhhhh,' Neville said. 'You can't break things, Rubella.'

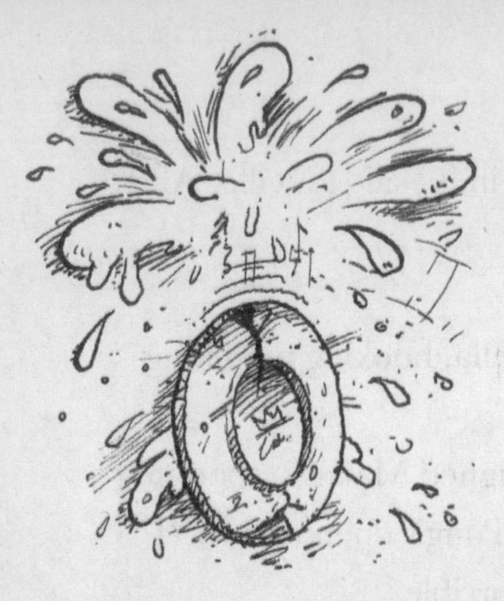

'I can,' growled Rubella and threw Neville's plate at the wall. It splattered all over the wallpaper.

'NO!' shouted Neville as Pong burst into excited laughter.

'Don't fret, Nev,' said Malaria. 'It's polite to smash your plate after eatin' . . . I think.'

'Yeah, Nev,' said Clod. 'Trollidays are all about funly, jiggish-type things like this. There's no harm done.'

Neville groaned. They just didn't understand.

'You can't break anything else and you've got to be quiet. My grandma Joan is coming to stay and she mustn't find out you're here.'

'Oh, lummy,' said Clod. 'We're going to meet the relatives –'

'No!' Neville interrupted. 'Grandma Joan is a nasty old bat. She'd have you stuffed and mounted on a wall if she could. It's her favourite hobby. She's meaner than a slurch.'

He told them the story of Grandma Joan and

the fox. And the one about her biting the milkman because he brought full-fat milk instead of semi-skimmed. And the terrible way she set the hounds on anyone who turned up unannounced.

'Well, how 'bout that?' Clod said, pulling a face. 'A scary overling? I never heard of such a thingummy. Have you, Belly?'

Clod turned to where Rubella had been sitting, but she wasn't there.

'That's odd,' said Malaria. 'She was there a teeny ticker ago.'

Neville had been so lost in his horror stories about Grandma Joan he hadn't even noticed Rubella leave. She must have been gone for a while.

'Where's she got to?' said Clod. His question was answered by the clomp of heavy feet and the *whoooooooosh . . . whoooooooosh* of the bathroom taps upstairs.

'She's running a bath,' said Neville, scratching his head. Somehow it didn't sound right.

'Belly?' chuckled Clod. 'Havin' a scrub?'

'That's a bit wonky,' said Malaria. 'Belly doesn't wash.'

'You're right,' said Neville. 'She can't be. She

wouldn't even fit in the tub.'

'Well, if she ain't havin' a bath,' Malaria thought out loud, 'why's she been runnin' those taps?'

'Oh, pook,' said Clod. Neville didn't like the sound of it. Clod was pointing to the holiday magazine lying open on the table.

There, in big blue letters, above a picture of children swimming and splashing, it said:

Meanwhile

Grandma Joan seized her cane in her gnarled hand and smacked the driver on the back of the head. He swerved and the car almost crashed.

'How much longer?' she hissed. 'The sooner we get there, the sooner we can leave.'

Joan sat back and sipped her champagne.

'Oh, and, driver,' she said, whacking him one last time for good measure, 'if you see any rabbits or squirrels, try and run them over. Oh . . . and if you come across any pedestrians, try to get some of those too. I love the way they go *bump-squelch*.'

Rubella's Swimming Pool

Neville had never run so fast in his life. He raced up the stairs, jumping two and three steps at a time, with Clod and Malaria galumphing after him.

'Rubella!' Neville yelled, banging his fists on the door. He could hear the *whooshing* of water and his troll-sister singing on the other side. '*Rubella!*'

'Belly!' shouted Clod from behind Neville. 'I'm not sure this is such a jubbly idea.'

'You get your bummly-bits out here right now!' Malaria ordered.

Neville started to panic. There was already water running out from beneath the door and trickling down the stairs. How long had Rubella had the water on?

'Rubella, please!' Neville yelled. He banged

again, but it was no use.

'Can't hear you!' Rubella shouted above the noise. Then she started singing. Neville couldn't hear too well, but it went something like this:

'*SPLISH, SPLASH, SPLOSH!*

I'VE HAD SOME NOSH

AND NOW I'LL 'AVE A SWIM . . .

AND IF THAT GRUB

SPOILS MY RUB-A-DUB-DUB,

I'LL DROP A ROCK ON HIM.'

'Here,' said Clod, swinging Neville on to his back so he could look through the window above the door. 'What's she up to?'

Neville stood on Clod's shoulders and looked down into the bathroom. It was worse than he thought. Rubella hadn't just turned the bath and sink taps on, she'd pulled them off completely. Water was gushing out of the broken pipes and was already halfway up the walls – and rising. Rubella was lying on her back, floating in the middle of the room alongside all sorts of shampoo bottles, toothbrushes and Neville's rubber duck.

'GURGLE, BUBBLE

NEV'S IN TROUBLE!'

'Stop it!' Neville shouted through the glass. 'You'll flood the whole house.'

'*SPLASH AND SPLOSH*,

FUN AND PLAY;

I'LL WASH YOUR STUPID

HOUSE AWAY!'

Rubella looked up at him and stuck out her tongue, then started doing the backstroke in little circles round the room.

'What did you say, scab?' she teased. 'I can't hear you.'

Neville pounded on the glass above the door, yelling his troll-sister's name. With one final shove, the window suddenly flapped inwards on its rusty hinges and he toppled head first into the water.

For a moment, Neville couldn't tell which way was up and which was down as he kicked and floundered in a storm of little bubbles. He tried to reach out and grab something to steady himself, but all he got was a squishy toilet roll and the pair of tweezers that Marjorie plucked her nose hair with.

'GET OUT!' Rubella screamed, grabbing Neville and hauling him up above the water. 'This is MY swimming pool.'

Neville spluttered. He could hear Clod and Malaria on the other side of the door banging and yelling.

'Y'right, Nev?'

'What's occurinating?'

Rubella splashed water in Neville's face.

'You're ruining my trolliday, you dungle dropping.'

Downstairs, Marjorie stomped back into the living room. She'd given up trying to get Herbert out from the cupboard under the sink. He was still there and refusing to budge. She looked at the soufflé splat that was running down the wall and the smashed plate on the floor. Those trolls were in for it now. Marjorie stormed towards the hole in the wall.

'Pull the plug!' Neville shouted to Rubella. 'We have to get the water out!'

Rubella splashed more water at Neville and snorted.

'Don't tell me what to do, you snot.'

'You have to!' Neville cried. He wasn't a very strong swimmer and was starting to sink.

Malaria, on the other side of the door, began to get angry.

'Right, you bonksome little madam!' she bellowed to her daughter. '*ENOUGH!*'

With that, Malaria gave the door handle an almighty yank. There was a loud creak, followed by a thunderous *GLUG* as the whole bathroom door came off in her hands.

Marjorie came through the hole in the wall and looked up the stairs to the landing. She saw Clod pounding on the wall and Malaria pulling at the bathroom-door handle. She opened her mouth to speak . . . and . . .

What Marjorie wanted to say was 'WHO DO YOU THINK YOU ARE? HOW DARE YOU COME HERE AND RUIN MY LOVELY HOUSE, YOU ROTTEN, STINKING BRUTES. GET OUT! GO ON – GET OUT!'

What actually came out of her mouth was something closer to 'BLAAAAAAAAAAAAHHHHH!' when she saw a wave as high as the ceiling plunging down the stairs with Malaria and Clod surfing on the bathroom door like a ride at a theme park.

'Look out, Margarine!' shouted Clod as he and Malaria caught hold of the banister and clung on as the water raged past them.

The wave roared like some fierce watery monster, taking picture frames and bath towels with it as it surged down the stairs. Neville shot out through the bathroom door, flapping his arms and kicking his legs. He tried to shout, but vanished beneath the churning water as it sped towards his mum.

Marjorie turned and ran towards the front door, screaming like a baby. No sooner had she opened it than the wave hit her and sent her shooting across the front garden like a soggy bullet from a house-shaped gun.

Marjorie landed with a *sploosh* on the lawn.

She wriggled on to her belly, then yelped as Neville landed on top of her with an almighty 'OOOOOOMMPH!'

Marjorie was just about to give him the smacked bottom of a lifetime when she saw a pair of very prim, very shiny black leather boots. She followed the skinny ankles upwards . . . grey stockings . . . a woollen, peacock-blue coat . . . sparkly rings on every gristly finger . . . an elegant old fox fur . . . pointy horn-rimmed glasses and a scowl to match Rubella's . . .

Grandma Joan peered down at Marjorie and Neville like they were worms in the dirt.

'Revolting,' she said.

Grandma Joan

'Hello, Grandma,' Neville said. His slippers were full of water and made rude slurpy noises as he scrabbled to his feet.

Joan flinched as if even the sound of his voice hurt her ears.

'Shut up, you little wart,' she hissed. 'Children should be like stuffed animals. Very still and very silent.'

Marjorie coughed politely.

'What –' Joan said, lifting Marjorie's chin with the point of her cane – 'are you doing?'

'Joan!' Marjorie jumped up and tried to give the old woman a hug. 'We were just . . . um . . . gardening . . . in the dark.'

Joan whipped her cane out and barred Marjorie's way. 'Come any closer in those wet clothes and I'll throw you head first into the tumble-drier, d'you hear?' she said. 'You people are strange, and strange people upset my nerves.'

Neville stared at his grandma. In the light of the street lamps she looked like a mummy that had lost its bandages. Her hair was like silver wire and her skin was thin and foldy like old paper. She had the permanent expression of someone sucking on a super-sour sweet.

'Well?' said Grandma Joan. 'Are you going to show me inside or do I have to stand out here all night?'

The old woman shoved between Neville and Marjorie and stalked up the garden path towards the front door, her cane clicking and splishing on the gravel as she went.

Neville stuck his tongue out at his grandma's back as she tottered towards the house like an angry stick insect. She always visited at the same time every year and she was always meaner than the last time.

'You old bat,' Neville whispered to himself. He wished Captain Brilliant were there. That mean weasel wouldn't stand a chance against someone like Captain Brilliant. He'd boot her in the backside and send her packing in no time.

'*Uuhhgh,*' Marjorie suddenly grunted. She was pointing towards the house with the kind of look that belonged on the face of someone who had just swallowed a hive of bumblebees.

Neville saw what his mum had spotted and gasped.

The front door was wide open and he could plainly see Clod and Malaria climbing off the banister and coming down the stairs.

What was he going to do? Grandma Joan was heading straight towards them. In a few seconds, she'd look up. Even a blind old fossil like Joan couldn't miss two enormous trolls lumbering in her direction. She'd call the police or wake up all the neighbours with her screaming, or drop down dead with shock, or worse, hunt the Bulches down and have them turned into troll-skin rugs.

'WAIT,' wailed Marjorie. 'I must give my favourite mother-in-law a proper hug!' She grabbed the old woman by the scruff of the collar, spun her round and threw her arms and legs round Joan's middle.

Joan whacked her daughter-in-law with her stick and wriggled, but Marjorie held tight.

'It's so lovely to see you,' Marjorie sobbed,

bursting into pretend tears.

'GET OFF ME, YOU SOGGY IDIOT!'

Over Joan's shoulder, Marjorie pointed to Neville and then the house.

'Go!' she whispered. '*Run!*'

Neville darted up the path and in through the front door.

'Oh, there you are, Nev,' said Clod cheerily. 'Thought you'd wash up at some point. That was a sploshly old time, eh?'

'Not now,' puffed Neville. 'Grandma Joan has arrived.'

'Who?' said Malaria, pulling a dripping toilet brush out of her hair.

'My grandma Joan. Y'know – mean, nasty, vicious Joan.'

Malaria shrugged.

'She'll have you stuffed and turned into a sofa,' said Neville.

'I've never been a sofa,' said Clod. 'Sounds like fun.'

'*HIDE!*' shouted Neville, herding them up the stairs like cattle. He heaved and jabbed at their bottoms to get them moving faster.

'Watch where you're putting those pinchers,' said Clod, huffing and puffing ahead of Neville.

'Quick, Clod,' groaned Malaria. 'You're getting chunky as a lardy lumper.'

At the top of the stairs, they found Pong rolling and splashing in a puddle with the toilet seat round his neck and Rubella spread out on the bathroom floor like a beached whale in a yellow bikini.

'Quick, Rubella!' said Neville. 'You have to hide. Grandma Joan's here.'

'Don't tell me what to do, you little whelp,' she grunted. 'You've ruined my trolliday.'

'But you've got to hide,' Neville pleaded. 'Grandma Joan will skin you and turn you into a pair of gloves if she finds you.'

Confusion twitched across Rubella's face.

'Or stick your head on a wall, stuff it with straw and sew on little button eyes,' Neville carried on. 'That's what she's like.'

'There'll be no snacking at bedtime if you don't hurry up,' Clod threatened.

'Come on, Belly,' said Malaria as she picked Pong up from the floor. 'Now.'

They all bundled into Neville's bedroom and

slammed the door.

Neville switched the light off and listened. He heard Grandma Joan yelling and his mum cry out in surprise. She wasn't going to be able to hold Grandma Joan for much longer.

'Now keep quiet,' said Neville to the four troll-shaped shadows in the gloom, 'and don't move.'

He slipped back out into the hallway and closed the door behind him.

'What a disgusting mess,' came Joan's voice from downstairs. 'You did this on purpose, you rotten nincompoop.'

Marjorie ummed and ahhed, trying to think of an excuse.

'We're redecorating.'

'Why did my son marry you?' Joan said. 'You can't even keep a tiny hovel like this clean.'

Neville leaned back against the door, crossed his fingers and toes and prayed to Captain Brilliant that Joan didn't plan to stay for long.

Meanwhile

Joan glowered at a photograph of Herbert, Marjorie and their pathetic child in a frame above the fireplace. What a rotten little family. What were they up to? She could hear them whispering in the kitchen.

Joan flexed her fingers, making the knuckles crack loudly. 'Disgusting,' she mumbled.

She hated visiting her son . . . what was his name? Hubert? Harrold? Something like that . . . The only reason she still visited was because she enjoyed scaring them so much.

Joan huffed. What was that smell? At her age,

Joan's eyes and ears weren't what they used to be, but her nose never failed her. There was an odd scent in the air like something from a memory. It was a mix of mud, moss and old socks all rolled into one.

'Hmmmmmm,' Joan said quietly to herself. 'Interesting.'

Where's the Ceiling?

By the time Neville got back to his bedroom, it was past midnight. Grandma Joan had been horrible all evening, complaining and nitpicking, but at least the Bulches had stayed quiet and Joan had skulked off to bed none the wiser. Marjorie had made it very clear to Neville that he was in charge of their 'guests' and he had to keep them out of Grandma Joan's sight.

Inside his room, everything was dark. Neville could make out the shapes of Malaria fast asleep on his bed, Rubella snoring on the rug and Pong lying on a pile of stuffed toys. Where was Clod?

Neville tiptoed into the room. He was about to whisper his dooda's name in case he'd missed him in the shadows, when he noticed his bedroom window was wide open.

'Dooda?' Neville whispered as he reached the

window sill. The garden below was dark and shadowy, but Neville was pretty sure he'd be able to spot a hulking great troll if he was down there. 'Dooda?'

A grey-green arm suddenly appeared from above and wrapped itself round Neville's middle. Then, like it had done a long time ago in that rusty sewer pipe, it lifted him into the air.

Clod put Neville down gently on the roof next to him. He had his big grey-green knees tucked up under his chin and there were tears in his eyes.

'Hello, lump,' he said. 'You should be snizzling away in your dreams by now.'

'What's wrong?' asked Neville. He stretched as far as he could and put his little, short arm round Clod's neck. 'Why are you sad?'

'Oh, nonkumbumps,' said Clod. 'I'm not sad, silly. I'm all happy and jubbly. Look.' Clod pointed a finger into the night.

'What?'

'That!' Clod said, pointing with both hands.

'The sky?' asked Neville.

'I've never seen it before,' said Clod. 'When I was a wee nipster, my dooda told me all about you overlings not having a ceiling. Funny thing is . . . I never believed the old wotzit.'

'I hadn't thought of that,' said Neville. 'Those are stars . . . and that big thing there, that's the moon.'

'The moon,' said Clod. 'How blunking wonderbunk! I've always wanted to see the moon.'

'Well, now you have,' Neville said, hugging his dooda.

'Indeedy I have,' said Clod. 'Oh, but listen to me grizzling on. Why aren't you snoring and slumbersnortin'? Can't sleep?'

'No,' said Neville.

'Well . . .' Clod said, settling himself against the roof tiles. 'Why don't I tell you a snoozetime story?'

'OK.'

'Well, there's the story of the time Dribble Hacklebottom got her tongue caught on a frozen water pipe and had to stay there for a whole bang, bong and boom. Then there's the story of The Troll That Stole or the one about the plague of hinkapoots.'

Neville thought for a moment. 'Tell me about The Troll That Stole,' he said.

'Oh, that one,' chuckled Clod. 'She was a right nasty one was Lady Jaundice. She was a troll pirate – a truccaneer! D'you know that blighter broke into the Underneath left-sock store and stole every last one? She left us all starvatious, she did. It was ages till the next grab night and everyone got skinnier than a scrawner by the end.'

'That's horrible,' said Neville.

'Oh, you ain't wrong there,' said Clod. 'No one ever found her. She's still at large somewhere is old Lady Jaundice, the great big gonker.'

Neville yawned.

'But there's armfuls of time for stories later,' said Clod. 'You need your rest, lump.' He picked Neville up and stood with one foot on each side of the pointy roof. Neville didn't think he'd ever been so high up in his life and he liked it.

'I wonder what it's made of?' said Clod, glancing back at the sky once more.

'What?' asked Neville.

'The moon.'

'Oh. Some people think it's made of cheese,' said Neville.

'Toe cheese?' asked Clod, with a look of amazement.

'Maybe.'

'Jubbly,' said Clod. He gave Neville a little squeeze.

If either of them had looked down at that moment, they would have seen a small shadowy shape skittering across the lawn and vanishing into the bushes at the end of the garden. They might even have heard it cooing and laughing to itself, but they were far too distracted.

'Well, my little grub,' said Clod after a long

while. 'I think it's about time for a snooze.'

Clod swung down off the roof and into Neville's bedroom window.

'That,' whispered Clod, 'was squibbly.'

Clod put Neville down, planted a big kiss on the top of his head, and Neville wandered over to a pile of stuffed toys to lie down.

'Night, Nev,' whispered Clod as he settled himself on the floor next to the bed.

'Night, Dooda,' Neville yawned back. He'd forgotten that only moments before, someone else had been asleep on that same pile of toys.

AAAAAAAAAAGGGHH!

Neville woke with a start as Marjorie burst into his bedroom. She stood holding on to the doorframe like she was about to be sucked away.

'What's wrong?' he asked, rubbing the sleep out of his eyes.

'That wretched little thing has got out,' Marjorie said. 'It's all over the news.'

'What?'

'Never mind "WHAT?"' Marjorie snapped, half whispering, half grunting. She yanked Neville off the pile of toys. 'Quick!'

Neville ran downstairs to the living room. There were his dad and his mooma and dooda crowded round the television.

'What if Grandma Joan wakes up and sees everyone?' Neville gasped.

'S'all right, son,' Herbert said proudly. 'I popped

one of your mother's sleeping tablets in her tea last night. She'll snooze through to lunchtime easily. I think I did quite well really, if you ask –'

'Shut up, you ninny,' Marjorie said through gritted teeth. '*What are we going to do?*'

Rubella was slumped on the sofa, picking her nose and smirking. All three of his troll family were wearing thick sunglasses, even though the curtains were drawn.

'You're in big trouble, Nev,' Rubella chuckled.

'What's going on?' Neville asked. If Pong really had got out, anything could have happened to him by now.

'Looks like someone wasn't watching Pong like they were supposed to,' Rubella said. She flicked a fat bogey at him.

Neville pushed through Clod and Malaria, who were transfixed by the television. They'd never seen one that actually worked before. Neville wasn't sure whether they cared more about Pong being lost or the moving pictures on the screen. He reached out and turned the volume up as high as it would go.

There was Silvia Simmonds, the morning

newsreader, and behind her was a huge picture of Pong.

'Reports are coming in,' read Silvia, 'of a strange new creature that was found after it smashed the front window of a shoe shop and ate half the stock.'

'Oh, Pong does love a boot or two,' said Clod. He was snacking on a pair of Herbert's slippers himself. 'I should have checked he'd grunched a few before we came up here.'

'Shhh,' said Malaria, putting a hand over Clod's mouth. 'Listen, our little grubling is famous. I'm so proud I could boogle my bunions.'

'We now go live,' said Silvia Simmonds, 'to London Zoo, where the creature has been put on display.'

A freckly man with spectacles and bright ginger hair came on to the screen.

'Good morning, Silvia,' said the freckly, ginger-haired man. 'The creature is believed to be a new type of monkey-seal-pig. The first of its kind in fact.'

'A monkey-seal-pig?' said Neville.

'I know,' beamed Malaria. 'We've never had a monkey-seal-pig in the family before. I'm as chuffed as a chuffer.'

'Here at London Zoo, we're all very excited,' the ginger man continued. 'The monkey-seal-pig will be our star attraction for many years to come.'

Herbert turned the television off. 'Marvellous,' he said, rubbing his hands together contentedly. 'Pong in a cage for . . .'

'Years?' said Clod. 'Did that freckly-fuzzbonk just say "many years to come"?'

Neville nodded.

'They can't put our Pong in a cage for –' Malaria gulped – 'years.'

'Too right they can't,' said Marjorie from the doorway. 'People will soon get bored of the little blighter, and when they do, they'll come looking for more of you.'

'What?' said Malaria.

'You mark my words,' said Marjorie, wagging her finger at Malaria like she was a naughty schoolgirl. 'We'll have hordes of people here next, all wanting to meet a real-life troll.'

'Oh no,' said Malaria. 'This has bungled things right up. If we don't get our lumpling back, we'll have overlings snuffling and grippling us underlings all over the place. They might even wiffle down Underneath and . . . AND . . . TIDY UP!'

'It's not good,' said Clod. 'This is a right pickle.'

'Forget the little monster,' Herbert said to Neville, trying to look as stern as he possibly could. 'He was nothing but trouble right from the start.'

'We can't leave Pong in the zoo,' gasped Neville.

'It's none of our business,' said Herbert. 'That's final.'

'I blame Nev,' said Rubella, pointing a stubby finger at him. 'Let's put him in the zoo instead.'

You're On Your Own

'Well, I'm not having anything to do with it,' barked Marjorie. She clapped her hands together as if she were brushing off something dirty. 'Good riddance.'

'Your mum's right,' said Herbert.

'Your grandma will be awake soon,' Marjorie added. 'She'll want to be entertained and you've got it seriously wrong if you're expecting your father and I to do it alone. We need all the help we can get. Pong is NOT our problem.'

Herbert and Marjorie humphed off to the kitchen to drink tea and feel sorry for themselves. Neville pulled a face as they went. Suddenly he wished it was his mum and dad in a cage at London Zoo.

'This is dreadly,' said Clod. 'Our

little Pong is lost again. What are we going to do?'

'We need a brainy-bonker plan,' said Malaria.

'It's not going to be easy,' said Neville.

'Count me out,' Rubella scoffed, flicking through her *Happy Holiday* magazine.

'Belt up, Belly,' said Clod.

Rubella scowled. This trolliday was turning out to be rubbish.

There was a long silence . . . a very long silence.

'Any ideas?' Neville finally asked.

'We could . . . erm . . . umm,' said Malaria.

'How about . . . ? Well . . .' said Clod.

Neville racked his brain. What would Captain Brilliant do at a time like this? How were they going to break Pong out of London Zoo?

'Umm . . . Maybe we could try to –' Neville said, before Rubella suddenly jumped off the sofa and interrupted.

'I'LL DO IT!' she yelled.

'What?' said Malaria. 'You feelin' all right?'

'I've had a change of heart. I couldn't bear to see my little brother locked away and all alone. Poor little pluglet.'

Neville almost laughed. He didn't think Rubella

even had a heart to change.

'Let me go to London and get him,' Rubella begged. 'I'll run fast and keep out of sight, honest.'

'It's a blunking long way,' said Clod.

'I don't mind,' said Rubella. 'Neville can come with me to keep me company. He can ride on my shoulders.' Then she did the strangest thing Neville had ever seen. Rubella smiled at him.

Something wasn't right.

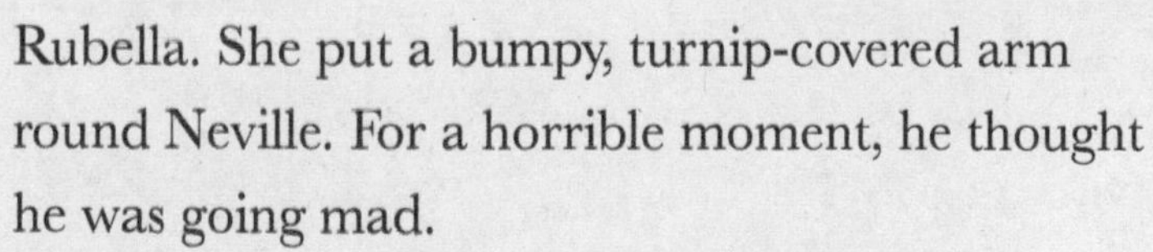

'We'll need a map,' said Neville nervously. He couldn't quite put his finger on what was wrong. 'There's one in my dad's car.'

'You're so clever,' said Rubella. She put a bumpy, turnip-covered arm round Neville. For a horrible moment, he thought he was going mad.

'Good for you, Belly,' said Clod with a grin. 'Whoever knew you could be so teamly.'

'I know,' said Rubella and batted her crusty eyelashes.

'First things first,' said Malaria. 'We need to

make a distraction so Belly and Nev can get our porklet back without Herburg, Margarine and that oversized squoggle of a grandma knowing. Any ideas, Nev?'

'Well, Grandma Joan likes to be complimented and she loves posh people,' said Neville.

'Hmmmm . . .' said Malaria, hatching an idea.

Rubella picked Neville up.

'Let's help Mooma and Dooda and then we'll go find that map,' she said.

Neville gulped. He hadn't noticed the rolled-up magazine in her hand that was turned to a page saying, '*WHY NOT GO FOR A SPIN IN THE COUNTRYSIDE?*'

Meanwhile

Grandma Joan reached for her cane, swung her gnarled old legs out of bed and hobbled blindly to the window. She put on her pointy glasses, peered out at the sunny morning weather and cursed. She never slept this late normally. Her head felt fuzzy like she'd drunk too much champagne.

'What a horrid night,' she snarled.

A small bird bobbed along the window ledge on the other side of the glass.

'Hmmmm,' Joan mumbled. She slowly edged the window upwards and held out a hand towards the little creature. 'Hello, you,' she said.

The little bird hopped forward and chirruped. Joan held her breath and waited very patiently until it was just inside the window sill . . . then,

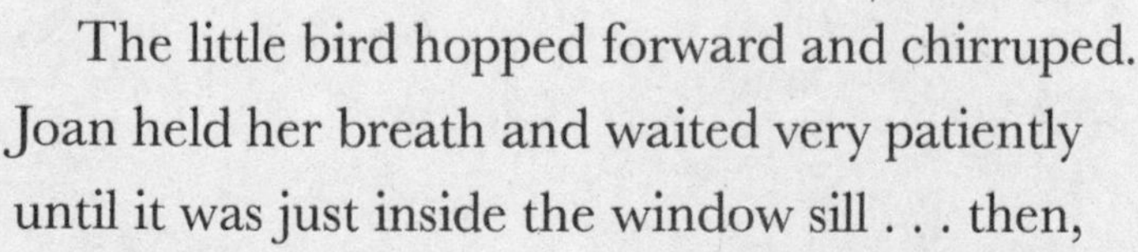

with a sickening laugh, she swung her cane like a golf club and thwacked it in a high arc across the garden. It landed in a dazed flurry of feathers and angry chirps in a flowerpot.

'How marvellous,' Joan chuckled. 'Bye bye, birdie.'

The Plan

'Erm, Mummy,' Herbert said nervously. 'We were thinking of going on an outing today. You know –'

'An outing?' Joan spat the words out. She had a headache.

'Yes,' said Herbert. 'There's the donkey sanctuary or the local hop farm. How about the pottery shop? You'd like that.'

'A pottery shop?' huffed Grandma Joan across the dining table. 'Why would I want to go and look around a boring, peasant-ridden little pottery shop?'

'I just thought it might be a nice idea, Mummy,' said Herbert. His bottom lip was quivering like a baby about to have a tantrum.

'Well, it's not,' Joan snapped and flung a piece of toast at him. It landed in his lap, jam-side down.

'I don't want to go anywhere.'

'There's the Stamp-collecting Museum,' said Marjorie. 'How does that sound?'

'Aaaaagh.' Joan picked up her cup of tea and emptied it over Marjorie's head. 'I travelled all this way to see you and all you seem to want to do is haul me off to a pottery shop or a stamp museum? HOW DARE YOU!'

'Well . . . erm,' said Marjorie, dripping wet for the second time in two days, but far too afraid to be angry. 'I . . . erm . . . I –'

'DAAARLINGS!' An enormous woman burst in through the living-room door. 'HOW ARE WE ALL?'

Marjorie and Herbert's jaws almost hit the table. It was Malaria. She was wearing a huge pink dress with puffy sleeves and a bustle that made her bottom look gigantic. Marjorie recognized the pattern on it straight away and fumed silently. It was made from her bedroom curtains.

Every bit of Malaria's grey-green skin was covered in Marjorie's expensive make-up and was now a lovely peach colour. She even had round, rosy cheeks, drawn-on eyelashes and dark red

lipstick. And . . . to top it all off, Malaria's bristly hair was crammed under a tall white wig made from what looked like scrunched-up toilet paper.

'Who are you?' croaked Joan, reaching for her cane to smack the stranger. She squinted to try and get a better look.

'I am . . . I am . . . Lady Bulch – ington.'

'Lady who?' Joan asked, quickly dropping her

cane and forcing her foldy face into a smile. This could be her chance to mingle with high society.

'Lady Bulchington,' said Malaria in a strange, high-pitched voice. 'I'm just visiting from my . . . erm . . . castle. I'm always searching for a posh, rich, better-than-everyone-else friend or two. I do tire of talking to common folk.'

'Well, you've come to the right woman,' Joan cheered, shoving Herbert and Marjorie out of the way.

'MARVELLOUS!' beamed Malaria. 'Won't you join me in a round of . . . of . . .'

'Croquet,' whispered Neville, who was huddled under Malaria's great dress like a camper in a tent.

'CROQUET!' shouted Malaria. 'Yes, I need a new . . . erm . . . Mistress of Croquet at my castle.'

'Well, it's certainly better than a stamp museum,' said Joan, shooting an evil glare at Herbert and Marjorie. 'Why didn't you tell me you lived near aristocrats?'

'Marvellous, m'dear,' Malaria giggled. 'You must meet my husband.'

'Husband?' whimpered Marjorie, trying very hard not to burst into tears.

'Why yes.' Malaria turned to the door with Neville desperately trying to avoid her big feet below. 'O HUSBAND O' MINE!'

'OH . . . DO BEG ME MY PARDONS, LADY AND GENTLEGEORGES.' Clod waltzed into the room, doing his best to be as overlingy as he could. He too had peachy skin and was wearing a long coat made from the rug in Neville's bedroom and . . . he wasn't bald.

Marjorie glared at the toffee-coloured wig sitting atop Clod's head and then almost fell off her chair in horror. It wasn't a wig, IT WAS NAPOLEON. The poor little thing was curled up on Clod's sweaty noggin and held in place with sticky tape.

'Aaaaaaagh!' Marjorie screamed. 'AAAAAAGH!'

'What's wrong with you?' Joan hissed. 'Do not embarrass me in front of the guests. This could cost me a damehood.'

Marjorie couldn't speak, so she just pointed at Clod's head and squeaked.

'OH, FORGIVE ME,' Clod said grandly. 'I NEVER INTRODUCTED MYSELF. I AM LORD CLODLY. PLEASURE TO MEET YOU, YOUR HIGHNESS.' Then he curtsied.

Neville peeked out from beneath Malaria's dress. Joan looked thrilled. How had she not noticed the difference between a huge pair of trolls covered in toadstools and a real lord and lady?

'Great job, Mooma,' whispered Neville. 'Now just keep her busy till we get back.'

'Course we will,' Malaria whispered to her dress. 'She reminds me a bit of old Gristle Pilchard.'

'Well, it's about time,' Joan said with a huge smile on her face. 'Finally some well-bred people. I was beginning to think I was surrounded by peasants and grubby urchins.'

Joan turned to Herbert and Marjorie, who were both still gawping like a pair of goldfish.

'WELL?' shouted Joan. 'Lord Clodly and Lady Bulchington want to play croquet.'

Marjorie shrugged and mumbled.

'To the garden!' Joan announced, waving her cane in the air and hobbling off to the kitchen and the back door.

'TO THE GARDEN,' Clod and Malaria joined in, grabbing Herbert and Marjorie and dragging them outside.

Neville scrabbled out of the back end of Malaria's tent dress as his mum, dad, mooma and dooda all trudged off to play croquet on the back lawn with Grandma Joan. It might not have been the sort of plan Captain Brilliant would have come up with, but by some absolute miracle, it had worked.

London Zoo . . . Here We Come

'I know it's here somewhere,' said Neville, searching under the passenger seat. 'My dad always keeps a map.'

'Well, look harder,' said Rubella from the driver's seat. She smiled to herself. While Neville wasn't looking, she'd already snatched the map and sat on it.

'It was here before, I know it was.'

'Oh well,' Rubella sighed. 'We'll just have to come up with another plan.' Then she quickly flicked the locks. Neville, who still had his head stuffed under the seat, heard the *clunk* and his heart froze.

'What are you doing?' He scrabbled back up.

Rubella held up the magazine for Neville to see.

'We're going for a drive,' she said with a wicked glint in her eye.

'NO. We can't,' said Neville, his eyes bulging

with fear. 'You don't know how to drive!' He quickly put his seat belt on. Rubella was going to get them both killed, he just knew it.

'I'll learn,' Rubella snapped. 'How do you make it go?' She clamped her sunglasses further down her nose. 'HOW DO YOU MAKE IT GO, SCAB?'

'Erm . . .' said Neville.

'C'mon,' she grumbled, holding tightly to the steering wheel with a crazed look on her face as if it were moving at top speed.

'You need to turn the key,' said Neville. 'But you can't do this, Rubella. If we get caught we'll be arrested and sent to prison.' He glanced down and almost screamed. The keys were already in the ignition. Herbert was always forgetting to take them out and now Neville had let Rubella know how to start the car.

'Don't be such a squirmer,' Rubella scowled. 'Mooma and Dooda have distracted your rotsome family and if anyone tries to stop us . . . I'll bash 'em.'

'Yes, but –'

'Shut your rat hole,' Rubella barked. She pulled Neville's seat belt and then let it go, making it snap back against his belly.

'Ouch!' wailed Neville. 'We have to work together, Rubella.'

Rubella reached down and turned the key. The engine juddered into life.

'I'm the one with the wheely thing,' she snarled. 'I'm in charge! What next?'

'I don't know,' Neville whimpered.

Rubella started growling.

'You have to push the pedals,' said Neville, rubbing the red seat-belt mark on his belly.

'Is that all?' said Rubella.

Neville nodded. His insides were bubbling and twitching and he felt sick with worry. Rubella would crash the car in no time. He closed his eyes and hummed the Captain Brilliant theme tune to himself.

'Right then,' said Rubella, as calmly as if she were just switching on the radio. 'LONDON ZOO, HERE WE COME!'

'NOOOOOOOOOOOOOOOOOOOOOO!!'

She slammed her pudgy foot down on to the pedal and the car screeched down the driveway and out into the road. They were heading straight for the house on the other side.

'TURN!' yelled Neville. 'TURN!'

At the last second Rubella spun the wheel and skidded off to the left, leaving tyre tracks on the grass of the house opposite. The car whizzed round and leapt back on to the road.

'Relax, Nev,' Rubella laughed at him. 'You're such a snivlet!' Rubella pushed the pedal down as far as it would go. 'We'll be there in no time.'

The car hurtled down the road like a rusty green comet.

'NEEEOOOOORRR!' Rubella made fast car sounds as she drove. 'BRRROOOORRRRMMM!'

The little green car weaved in and out of lamp posts and even other cars. It sped past Neville's school and the shops like a blur. Rubella didn't brake at the speed bumps, she just bounced over them instead.

'What's this do?' said Rubella and pushed the button on Herbert's fancy satnav gadget. The screen flickered on and a lady's voice said, 'Turn right in two hundred yards.'

'WHO ARE YOU?' she screamed at the little box.

'Turn right in one hundred and fifty yards.'

'NO!'

'Turn right in one hundred yards.'

'SHUT UP!'

'You have missed your turn-off.'

'I SAID SHUT UP!' Rubella grabbed the gadget from the dashboard, threw it over her shoulder and through the back windscreen.

Neville was starting to break out in a cold sweat. His dad loved that satnav box.

'GET OUT THE WAY!!' Rubella stuck her head straight through the glass of her window and yelled at a lollipop lady crossing the road. She dropped her lollipop sign and gawped back in disbelief at the troll face grimacing at her in a furious, speeding blur. 'ROADHOG!!!'

'That was Mrs Higgins, the lollipop lady for my school,' groaned Neville. He'd just have to hope she hadn't recognized him.

'Woo-hoo! This is squibbly,' Rubella laughed.

Neville was struck dumb with fear. He watched in horror as the car reached a roundabout. There were lots of other cars and motorbikes driving round it, but Rubella didn't care. She drove straight out and across the top of it, sending the other cars skidding in all directions.

'Who put that there?' she yelled.

Meanwhile

Lady Bulchington smacked the ball with her croquet mallet so hard that it flew about fifty metres into the air.

DONK . . . It bounced off the chimney.

SMASH . . . It shot through the greenhouse.

CLANG . . . It bounced off the dustbins and then landed only centimetres from where Herbert was standing with a dull *THUMP.*

'Well played, Lady Bulchington,' said Grandma Joan, beaming. 'What a squiffling swing you have.'

'BRAVOOOO!' yelled Lord Clodly.

Next was Grandma Joan's turn. She deliberately positioned herself just behind Marjorie and then swung the mallet as hard as she could at her head. *CLONK* . . .

'OOOOWWW!' yelped Marjorie, trying not to say something very rude.

'Haha . . . whoops!' Joan chuckled. 'How squibbly.'

Mungo the Monkey-Seal-Pig

They drove and drove and drove and drove and drove. By the time they reached London Zoo it was dark and the zoo was closed.

Rubella had driven the wrong way over Tower Bridge, crashed through the market stalls in Covent Garden and even stopped the car in the middle of Trafalgar Square to demand directions. Anyone she stopped ran away screaming in fear from the walrus in a yellow bikini.

'It's true what they say,' Rubella said to Neville as she got back in the car. 'People in London are so rude – dungle droppings!'

Finally, Neville peered through the gates. He couldn't quite believe he was still alive.

'It's awfully dark,' he whispered. 'What do we do now?'

'We go in,' said Rubella. 'That's why we came here, you nogginknocker.'

'Yes, but how?' said Neville.

'Like this.' Rubella walked straight towards the front gates and smashed right through them. 'Easy as dunking a dingo.'

Inside, the zoo was scary and Neville could feel the hairs on the back of his neck standing on end.

'I don't like this,' he whispered, huddling close to Rubella's bulging side.

'Get off,' snapped Rubella, shoving him away.

They walked past the reptile house, the gorillas and the pygmy hippos. It was so spooky. There were strange howls and shrieks and Neville could feel hundreds of eyes glimmering in the darkness as they shuffled along.

Rubella eyed the pygmy hippos greedily. 'I wonder what they taste like?' she said.

Further along past the bearded pigs and the fountains, they started to hear a strange noise. It was a kind of cooing sound with bits of giggling and yelling in between.

'That sounds like Pong,' said Neville. 'Quick!'

They ran towards the sound and finally, in the

square between the tigers, spider monkeys and the lions, they found a big round cage with a sign above it.

'*Mungo the Monkey-Seal-Pig*,' Neville read aloud. Pong was hanging upside-down from a rope inside the cage.

'BLLLLUUUUURRRRGGGGGG!' he blurted when he saw them. 'OOOOOORRRGGGHHH!'

Rubella stepped up to the bars and gave them a shake. They wobbled, but didn't snap.

'Hmmmm,' she said. 'These are made of strong ole stuff.'

'Can't you break them, Rubella?' asked Neville.

'Of course I can!' she snapped.

Rubella took a few steps back for a bit of a run-up and then flung herself at the cage. She hit the bars with a massive *THWACK*, but they didn't break. They didn't even bend.

Pong howled with glee.

'That's it!' grunted Rubella as she clambered to her feet, looking a little dazed. 'I've had enough of this.' Then she turned on her heels and ran away.

'RUBELLA!' shouted Neville. He couldn't believe it. After getting all the way here, the stupid knucklehead was running away just because she couldn't break the bars. What was he going to do now? Pong was still trapped in his cage and Rubella had abandoned him in the middle of London. Neville slumped down on to his bottom and started to cry. Why was everything so difficult?

SCCRREEEEEEEEEEEEEEEEEEEECCHH!

Neville looked up in alarm. Further down the

dark pathway he saw the headlights of a car sweep round the corner of the gorilla enclosure and head straight towards him.

'MOVE, NEV!' Rubella shouted through her broken window. 'SHIFT YOUR BOTTOM BITS OR GET FLATTENED!'

The car jerked into the air and smashed straight through a large fountain, but it didn't stop.

'GET READY!' screamed Rubella as the car careered into Pong's cage. The crash was deafening. An alarm went off and all the animals in the zoo woke up and started howling, bleating and roaring. Neville dived for cover as broken bars flew in all directions. His dad's car . . . all bashed up and dented . . . yikes!

Then nothing moved.

'Rubella?' Neville said to the steaming car. 'Are you OK?'

Nothing . . .

'Rubella?'

The driver's door swung open with an exhausted-sounding squeak and Rubella tumbled out.

'Ooops,' she mumbled, her eyes crossed and her hair standing on end as if she'd been electrocuted. 'Ooooh, stars.'

'You did it, Rubella!' cheered Neville. 'Look.'

Pong jumped up on to the bonnet of the car, chewing on a piece of metal bar.

'Bluuuuuuuhhhhhhh,' he cooed merrily. Then he tossed the fragment away, which then bounced off Rubella's head. 'Cooooooooooooo.'

Neville grabbed Pong and put him on to the back seat of the car.

'We have to get out of here!' he said. 'Do you think . . . erm . . . maybe I should drive?'

Rubella's eyes straightened instantly and she flicked Neville on the end of his nose. 'Not on your nelly,' she said.

The Longest Game in the World

Hours later, the car finally juddered on to the front lawn of the Brisket house. One of the back wheels was slightly bent, every window was broken and there was a lamp post buckled across the front bumper.

Rubella fetched Pong and carried him upstairs while Neville staggered through the kitchen and looked out of the windows to the back garden. Lady Bulchington and Lord Clodly were still playing croquet. He looked at the kitchen clock.

'Three o'clock in the morning!' Neville gasped. They had been playing since he'd left for London.

Neville ran out into the moonlit back garden.

'We simply *must* play one more game,' said Lady Bulchington to a very exhausted-looking Joan.

'I can't,' grunted Joan. 'I –'

'Did I mention that I'm best friends with the Queen?'

Joan bolted upright. 'Maybe one more game,' she said.

'MARVELLOUS,' chuckled Lord Clodly.

Neville dived behind his mooma's dress. 'We're back,' he whispered.

Malaria heaved a massive sigh of relief. 'About time,' she replied quietly. Then she turned to Grandma Joan. 'Ooopsy, I forgot . . . I already have a Mistress of Croquet. Silly me. Sorry. Better luck next time.' Then Malaria swished her dress dramatically in the old woman's direction. 'I'M OFF!'

Malaria grabbed Lord Clodly, who looked like he was about to fall asleep standing up, and rushed him through the house and up to Neville's bedroom.

Grandma Joan dropped her croquet mallet on Marjorie's toe.

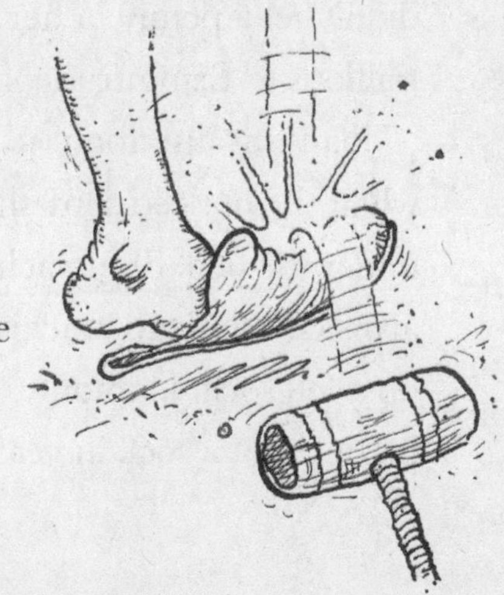

'This is your fault,' she hissed. 'You obviously made a bad impression. Now I'll never meet the Queen!'

Meanwhile

Joan had had enough. She was furious. All that wasted time playing croquet with Lord Clodly and Lady Bulchington.

She hobbled off to the spare room to call her driver to take her back to Brisket Hall, her lovely mansion house.

'This is Marjorie's fault,' she mumbled as she closed the spare-room door behind her. She'd get her revenge. Joan would make sure that Marjorie didn't get a penny in her will. She'd leave her millions to Ermintrude, her pet budgie, instead.

Joan was just about to pick up the telephone when she noticed something sticking out from under the bed. She reached down, her back and arms clicking and cracking as she went, and picked up a left sock. Joan only wore silk stockings and hadn't seen a sock in years and years.

She sniffed it curiously. 'Ooooooooooooooorrrh!'

Horror

'Oh, my jubbly little pluglet,' said Malaria and scooped Pong up. 'Your mooma's so proud of her monkey-seal-pig.'

'Absolunkly,' beamed Clod. 'And our little heroes here.' He put an arm round Neville and Rubella. 'Blunking marvellous.'

'Nev didn't do much,' huffed Rubella. 'Actually, he didn't do anything at all.'

'Well, he's still my hero,' said Malaria.

Neville loved being called a hero. He couldn't wait to tell Terrance and Archie at school on Monday. He'd be the coolest kid in town, he was sure of it. That is, until his dad saw the state of the car and grounded him for the next five hundred years.

'Right, my brandyburp,' Clod said to Malaria. 'Let's get out of these costumey things and have ourselves a nice left sock or two.'

'Indeedy, Clod, my lump.' Malaria put Pong down on the pile of toys and went to the mirror. 'All this make-up nonkumbumps,' she said. 'It's so oddly.'

Malaria spat on to a bath towel she'd snitched and rubbed at her face . . . then she rubbed a bit harder . . . then a bit harder.

''Ere, Nev,' she said. 'This make-up ain't comin' off.'

Neville jumped up from the bed and went to have a look. She was right. Malaria's face was still as peachy and rosy as ever.

'Try it again,' Neville said.

Malaria tried it again.

'Nothing,' she said.

That's when Neville noticed the towel. It was covered in make-up.

'Oh, pook,' said Neville.

'I don't like the sound of that, Nev,' said Clod, who was also scrubbing away with a corner of the bed sheet.

'Mooma,' Neville said gingerly. 'The make-up has come off. You're not wearing any.'

'What the –' Malaria turned back to the mirror, took one look at her lovely, peachy complexion and screamed.

'Don't you remember?' Neville shouted over the screaming. 'When I lived Underneath, I grew toadstools and my skin turned grey. You've been living up here. The same must have happened to you.'

'I can't be rosy,' Malaria wailed.

'We'll be fun-poked forever,' blurted Clod.

Rubella pointed and laughed at her parents.

'I don't know what you're laughing at, Belly,' Malaria whimpered. 'Where are your turnips?'

Rubella looked at her shoulders, saw that the turnips had vanished, then threw her head back and howled.

'NOOOOOOOOOOOOOOOOOOOOOOOOO-OOOOOO!'

Clod lifted Napoleon, who had given up wriggling and was now snoring peacefully, off his head and ran to join Malaria at the mirror. There, where Napoleon had been curled up, was a head of glossy brown hair.

'AAAAAAAAAAAAAAAGH!' yowled Clod.

Malaria grabbed at her toilet-paper wig and yanked it off.

Neville gasped.

Instead of Malaria's thorny bristles, there flopped a beautiful hairdo of long golden locks. They dangled all the way down her back and glistened in the dim light.

Malaria started tearing around the room and swatting at herself as if she were covered in hundreds of tiny, biting ants. Neville had to leap into the cupboard to avoid her. 'AAAAAAAAAA-AAAAAAAAAAAAAAAAAGGHH!'

She jumped on the bed and demolished it.

'AAAAAAAAAAAAAAAAAAAAAAGGHH!'

She ran straight through the wall into the hallway.

'AAAAAAAAAAAAAAAAAAAAAAGGHH!'

She kept running and in a blind panic burst through the wall into the spare bedroom where Grandma Joan was staying.

Malaria froze in her tracks. She stopped screaming and gawped at the scene before her. Neville ran in after her and gasped.

There was Grandma Joan sitting on the end of

the bed with a half-eaten left sock dangling from her mouth.

Secrets

'I knew there was something funksome about you,' Malaria said, pointing a stubby finger. Joan stared back like a rabbit in the headlights of a car. 'What's this all about?'

Clod, Rubella and Neville's mum and dad reached the doorway.

'Well, I'll be bungled,' said Clod.

Grandma Joan gobbled down the rest of the sock and peered through her spectacles at Malaria. On the Mooma's left shoulder was a large rip and one last remaining toadstool was poking out of it.

'TROLLS!' Joan shrieked. 'OF COURSE! Lady Bulchington and Lord Clodly? I should have known. I smelled you the minute I stepped in through the front door!'

'What's going on?' said Neville.

'How'd you know about trolls?' asked Marjorie.

'Mummy,' said Herbert. 'Is everything all right?'

'No, it blunkin' ain't,' interrupted Clod.

'She's one of us. She's an underling,' said Malaria.

'WHAT?' gasped Herbert. 'My mummy is not a dirty, stinking troll, if that's what you're trying to say.'

'OH, SHUT UP, YOU LITTLE FOOZLE FART!' Joan shouted at Herbert. 'OF COURSE I AM – WELL . . . WAS.'

'HA!' Rubella burst out laughing.

'I've just been up here too long, which by the looks of things so have you,' Joan continued, pointing at the Bulches. 'I turned all overlingy . . . smooth skin and no turnips . . . bleeeuuucchh . . . disgusting!'

'But you can't be!' blubbed Herbert. 'You're my mummy.'

'I'm not your mummy.' Joan scowled. 'I ate your mummy.'

Herbert turned green.

'Only kidding,' Joan chuckled. 'I had your

mumsie made into a pair of shoes with a matching handbag when you were a wee nipster.'

Then Herbert turned white.

'It c-can't b-be true,' he stammered.

'Of course it's not true, you grunty-gawper. I'm your mother,' said Joan, picking at a piece of sock in her teeth. 'You, m'boy, are half troll.'

Herbert looked like he was going to be sick.

'NOOOO!' he bawled. 'TELL ME IT'S NOT TRUE! TELL ME YOU HAD MY MUMMY MADE INTO A PAIR OF SHOES WITH A MATCHING HANDBAG . . . *PLEASE!*'

'You are half a troll, boy,' Joan said. 'There's underling blood in you. Get used to it.'

'Who are you?' said Malaria, getting angry and tossing her golden hair. 'A troll would never leave the Underneath for good. Why'd you come up here in the first place?'

'I had to escape,' Joan smirked. 'Don't you recognize me?'

Clod and Malaria glanced at each other. Their memory was so bad. They'd have no chance of recognizing a troll that didn't look like a troll any more.

Neville glared at the old woman. He wasn't sure, but now he thought about it, there was something vaguely familiar about her. That wrinkled, foldy face, her nose like a pointed carrot. He balled his hands into fists. *Think, Neville, think . . .*

'I knew you wouldn't be able to tell who I was,' Joan chuckled. 'You're all so stu–'

'I'VE GOT IT!' Neville shouted. He suddenly remembered Clod's story on the roof, and the day that Clod and Malaria had taken him for a trip round the town of Underneath. Clod had showed Neville a statue of Lady Jaundice. 'YOU'RE THE TROLL THAT STOLE!'

Rubella and his mooma and dooda all gasped.

'Lady Jaundice,' said Clod. He looked starstruck. 'Good gracicles.'

'I should've known one of you lot would come

up here for a trolliday at some point,' sneered Jaundice.

'NOOOOO!' yelled Herbert suddenly. 'You're telling me that not only is my mummy a grotty troll, she's a criminal as well?'

'It's your lucky day,' Rubella giggled.

'Well,' said Lady Jaundice, straightening her peacock-blue coat and grabbing her favourite fox fur. 'I'd love to dangle about and chat with you bunch of snots, but I have far more important things to do at my mansion. The chef is preparing roast kitten stuffed with caviar as we speak.'

With that, Joan blew a kiss at them and jumped head first towards the window.

Into the Underneath

'Oh no, you don't,' boomed Malaria, lunging forward. Jaundice had already smashed the window and was scrabbling out, but Malaria caught hold of her ankles and dragged her back inside with a bump. 'You ain't going anywhere. Half of Underneath would like to get their hands on you!'

'GET OFF!' Jaundice yanked her ankles free and started kicking and flailing wildly. 'NO ONE STANDS BETWEEN ME AND ROAST KITTEN!'

She flung her walking stick across the room, almost hitting Marjorie in the face. Her string of pearls snapped and clattered to the floor in a shower of little white droplets and the fox fur flew through the air and landed on Pong's head. He cooed loudly and pulled it into little pieces.

'Stop squiggling, you squirmer,' Malaria grunted, grabbing Jaundice round the waist and holding on tightly. 'I'm takin' you to prison.'

'Don't let go, Mooma,' Neville shouted over the din.

'YEAH,' Rubella joined in. She was laughing so hard, it looked like she might be in danger of wetting her hippo-sized pants. 'Squeeze the old gurnip.'

'My mother is NOT a gurnip!' Herbert snapped at Rubella. Then he turned to Neville. 'What's a gurnip?'

But Neville wasn't listening. He watched with a mixture of fear and excitement as Jaundice picked Malaria up and threw her at the wall. Malaria crashed through it like a wrecking ball on the end of a crane and landed in the bathroom with a loud 'OOOOOOOF!' Neville's eyes were practically popping out of his head. Who knew his grandma Joan was so agile and strong?

'MY HOUSE!' Marjorie screeched. 'STTOOOPPPP!'

'MY MUM!' Herbert squeaked, even higher than Marjorie. 'AAAAAAGH!'

'You grumping old glumper,' Clod shouted. He snatched up the bedside lamp and brandished it at Jaundice like a sword. 'Let's see who's the strongly one now!'

Jaundice laughed a high-pitched, insane, granny-type laugh and leapt towards the ceiling as Clod hurtled towards her. She swung over his head on the bedroom light and landed on the bed with a sickening crunch of old joints and bones.

Before Clod had even realized it, he ran straight through the outside wall and vanished into the night air. Neville gasped in horror as his dooda tumbled into the darkness. Everybody (including Jaundice) held their breath. There was a moment of silence, followed by the sound of an enormous splash, as Clod landed in the fish pond.

'Thank goodness!' Neville heaved a sigh of relief.

'Serves him right,' Jaundice growled from the bed. 'The great whelp.'

'RIGHT!' Malaria bellowed, sticking her head through the massive hole in the bathroom wall.

'You asked for it . . . GET HER, RUBELLY!'

Rubella, who had been watching from the doorway with a huge grin on her face, suddenly jumped into action.

'MOVE!' she snapped, shoving Neville, Herbert and Marjorie aside. Then she pointed at Jaundice. 'I'll squish you like mouldy potato, you . . . you –'

It was too late. Jaundice leapt from the bed and flew straight over Rubella.

'Stop jumping about, you old snot!' Rubella screamed, swatting at the air above her head. 'Stand still and let me squish you.'

'Not on your nelly, you womping great chunker,' said Jaundice. She landed behind Rubella and booted her in her enormous backside, sending her flopping on to the bedroom rug. Then, quicker than Neville had ever seen his grandma move before, she darted past him and ran into the hallway.

'Mummy,' whined Herbert. 'Come back.'

'Don't let her get away,' Rubella grunted. 'QUICK!'

Neville ran out of the room just in time to see his grandma skittering into the bathroom. There was the sound of clattering and smashing and then Malaria tumbled out into the hall.

'She's going to flush herself!' Malaria yelled, scrabbling back to her feet. 'Quick, Nev!'

Neville reached the bathroom door and stopped. Herbert and Marjorie appeared behind him, panting and whimpering. The three of them gawped at the half-troll-half-grandma thing standing with one foot inside the toilet bowl and her hand poised just above the flush.

'Mummy,' said Herbert. 'What about me?'

'Who cares about you?' the old troll gloated. 'I'd rather take my chances down there than stay here with you bunch of muck suckers. I'm Lady Jaundice, the marauder of the mud-beds, the fiend of the fungus forests –'

'The duchess of the dungle droppings,' Rubella shouted through the hole in the wall.

'I'M THE TROLL THAT STOLE AND YOU WON'T STOP ME!' Jaundice screamed. Then she pulled the flush and vanished down the toilet with a great surge of water.

'What are we going to do now?' asked Neville.

'Well, you've got another think coming if you expect me to go down there after –'

Marjorie hadn't even finished her sentence when – 'Yip,yip . . . yiiiippp!' – Napoleon scampered between her legs, sprang up on to the toilet seat and with one final 'Yiiiiippp!' jumped in after Jaundice.

'MY BABY!' Marjorie howled. Without a second's thought, she flew across the bathroom and dived head first into the toilet bowl. Neville could still hear her screaming as her fluffy pink slippers disappeared round the U-bend.

'Oopsy,' said Malaria. 'That were unexpected.'

'What did I miss?' Clod reached the top of the stairs. He was dripping wet and covered in pondweed. 'Where's the old glumper?'

'She flushed herself, and now my mum has just gone down the pipes after Napoleon,' said Neville frantically. 'We have to go after her!'

'Nev's right,' Malaria said, far too casually to reassure Neville. 'If she misses the lantern pipe, she's in trouble.'

'WHAT?' shouted Herbert.

'S'pose that's the end of our trolliday then?' said Clod. He pulled a glum face, picked up a newt from his shoulder and popped it into his mouth. 'What a shame. I was enjoyin' that, I was.'

'COME ON!' Herbert shouted again. His face was getting redder and redder. 'You have to go after them!'

'All right, Hergberg,' said Clod. 'Don't get your panty-bloomers in a twizzle.' Clod picked Herbert up and swung him on to his back. 'Deep breath now, Herb.'

Herbert sucked in a huge bellyful of air and held it with a look of utter terror on his face.

'Here we go,' said Clod. He placed a spade-sized foot into the toilet and pulled the flush.

Neville could hardly believe the things he'd seen in the past ten minutes. First his grandma turning out to be a notorious thieving troll, then his dog and mother jumping down the loo and now his dad vanishing after them on the back of his hulking great dooda.

'Right, Nev,' said Malaria. 'We'd better follow.' Just like the others, she put one foot into the toilet then waggled the other one towards Neville. 'Grab on.'

Neville grabbed hold of Malaria's thick ankle. Then Rubella waddled into the room and wrapped her arm round Neville's waist, and Pong clung to Rubella's turnip-free back.

'Get on with it,' grunted Rubella. 'I don't want to miss what happens.'

Neville held his breath.

Here we go again, he thought as Malaria pulled the flush and the four of them shot off down the pipes like a strange and very grisly Christmas paper chain.

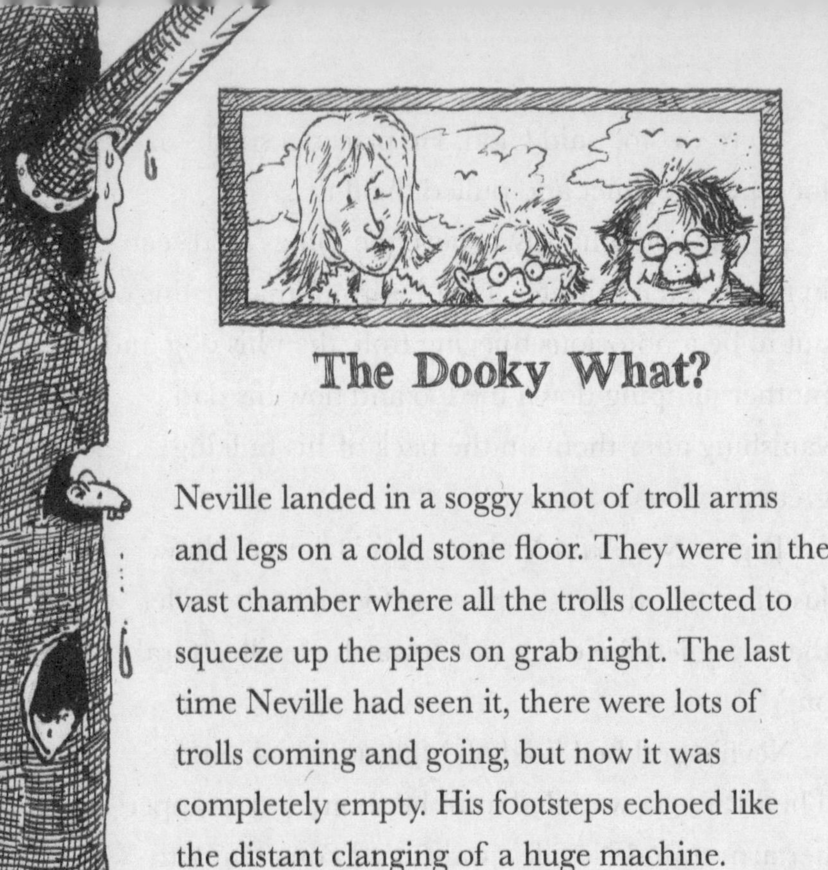

The Dooky What?

Neville landed in a soggy knot of troll arms and legs on a cold stone floor. They were in the vast chamber where all the trolls collected to squeeze up the pipes on grab night. The last time Neville had seen it, there were lots of trolls coming and going, but now it was completely empty. His footsteps echoed like the distant clanging of a huge machine.

'C'mon then, we've got catching up to do.' Malaria swung Pong on to her back and nudged Rubella to her feet.

'All right,' Rubella grunted. Neville noticed that turnips had already started to sprout across her shoulders again.

'Your dooda must have gone further down the pipes, past the lantern tunnels,' said

Malaria as a toadstool suddenly grew from the side of her neck. 'If your mumsie got washed past that, there's only one place she could be.'

'Where?' asked Neville.

'The dooky hole,' said Malaria, pulling a face.

Neville gulped.

Rubella laughed.

'Please tell me that's a really nice part of the Underneath,' said Neville.

'Erm, not exactly,' Malaria smiled nervously. 'I think we'd better run.'

Neville's feet kept slipping on the slimy floor as they ran, and the smell was awful. He heard Marjorie's wailing before they even got to the dooky hole. He was going to have to do the washing-up for the rest of his life after this. He just knew it.

'Not far now, Nev,' Malaria said as she led the way through a maze of tunnels that became grimier and grimier with every step they took. She was covering her nose to keep out the stink. This was REALLY BAD. If even trolls had to cover their noses, the dooky hole must be the most disgusting place in the universe.

They rounded a bend and walked into a cramped stone room. Neville squinted to see, it was so gloomy.

'Grab on,' came a voice. 'Stop being a gonk and take hold of the string.' It was Clod and Herbert bent over what looked like a wishing well. Clod was holding a fishing rod and dangling it down inside the well. 'Come on, Margarine!'

'What is this place?' Neville asked Malaria. His eyes were watering from the revolting stench in the air.

''Orrible place, this,' she said, kicking aside a stray toad. 'Down that well is where all the nasty bits in the sewers wash up. Even trolls don't come to these parts without a blunkin' good reason.'

Neville ran to the edge of the dooky hole and looked down. He couldn't see anything.

'Come on, Mum!' he shouted.

Rubella started giggling again.

'Quickly, darling,' whined Herbert. 'I don't like it down here.'

There was a sudden tug on the string and Clod

yanked the fishing rod up and away from the hole. 'Just you wait, Margarine,' he chuckled. 'We'll have you clean and squibbly in no time.'

Bit by bit, Clod reeled in the fishing line. Neville could hardly bear to look as Marjorie slowly emerged from the dooky hole. Clod's fishing hook had caught her pink blouse by the back of the collar and she dangled there like a human-sized mud pie clinging to a tiny Napoleon-sized mud pie. Every bit of her was smeared in thick grey sludge and there were globs of rubbish and fish guts, and other things that Neville didn't even want to think about, stuck to her.

'Mmmm . . . blurgle . . . buh . . . blah . . . boooh . . .' Marjorie spluttered.

'What's she sayin'?' asked Rubella.

'Blug . . . m'bluh . . . groob . . . blum . . . bluh . . .'

'I don't know,' said Clod. 'But she's a lot heavier than she looks.'

'Blooo . . . buh . . . m'burgle . . . buh . . .'

Marjorie's mouth was filled with slime and mud. Her eyes kept darting downwards and her hands flapped crazily up and down.

'Are you all right, sugar blossom?' said Herbert. He pulled a small tube of antibacterial spray from his pocket. 'Would you like some?'

Marjorie swatted Herbert away and spat out a mouthful of sludge, hitting Rubella in the face with a sticky slap. Pong clapped and cooed wildly.

'SHE'S GOT HOLD OF MY FEET!' Marjorie shrieked.

'Huh?' Clod yanked the fishing rod higher into the air and a second human-sized mud pie flopped out of the hole.

'MUMMY!' Herbert said. 'Is that you?'

A very grotty Jaundice jumped up and snarled at

the unlikely gaggle of trolls and people before her.

'Don't you ever give up?' she grunted.

'YOU!' said Malaria, rubbing her hands together. 'I'm not finished with you.'

'Oh yes, you are,' cackled Jaundice. She ran out of the stone room and up the passageway that led back to the pipe chamber.

'GET HER!' yelled Clod, throwing the fishing rod aside. He galumphed out of the room.

'Quick!' Neville ran after Clod.

'Mummy!' Herbert ran after Neville.

'Oh, pook!' Malaria ran after Herbert.

'Not again!' Rubella ran after Malaria.

'Oooooorrgh!' Pong ran after Rubella.

'Yip . . . yip . . . splutter . . . yip!' Napoleon ran after Pong.

'MY BABY!!' Marjorie ran after Napoleon.

And they all ran after Lady Jaundice.

The Getaway

Neville caught up with Clod as they ran down tunnels and up pipes, across bridges and under archways.

'Keep going, Nev,' Clod wheezed. He wasn't the fittest of trolls.

Ahead, Neville could see Jaundice skittering along at an alarming speed. She'd spent so much time away from the Underneath that she was changing almost instantly. Her silver hair was twisting and crackling into thick briary branches and she was growing taller and wider with every step. Instead of toadstools, she had carrots sprouting out through her coat across her neck and shoulders. Their green tops bobbed and flapped as she ran.

'She's heading for the town,' wheezed Clod between heavy gasps of air. He was right.

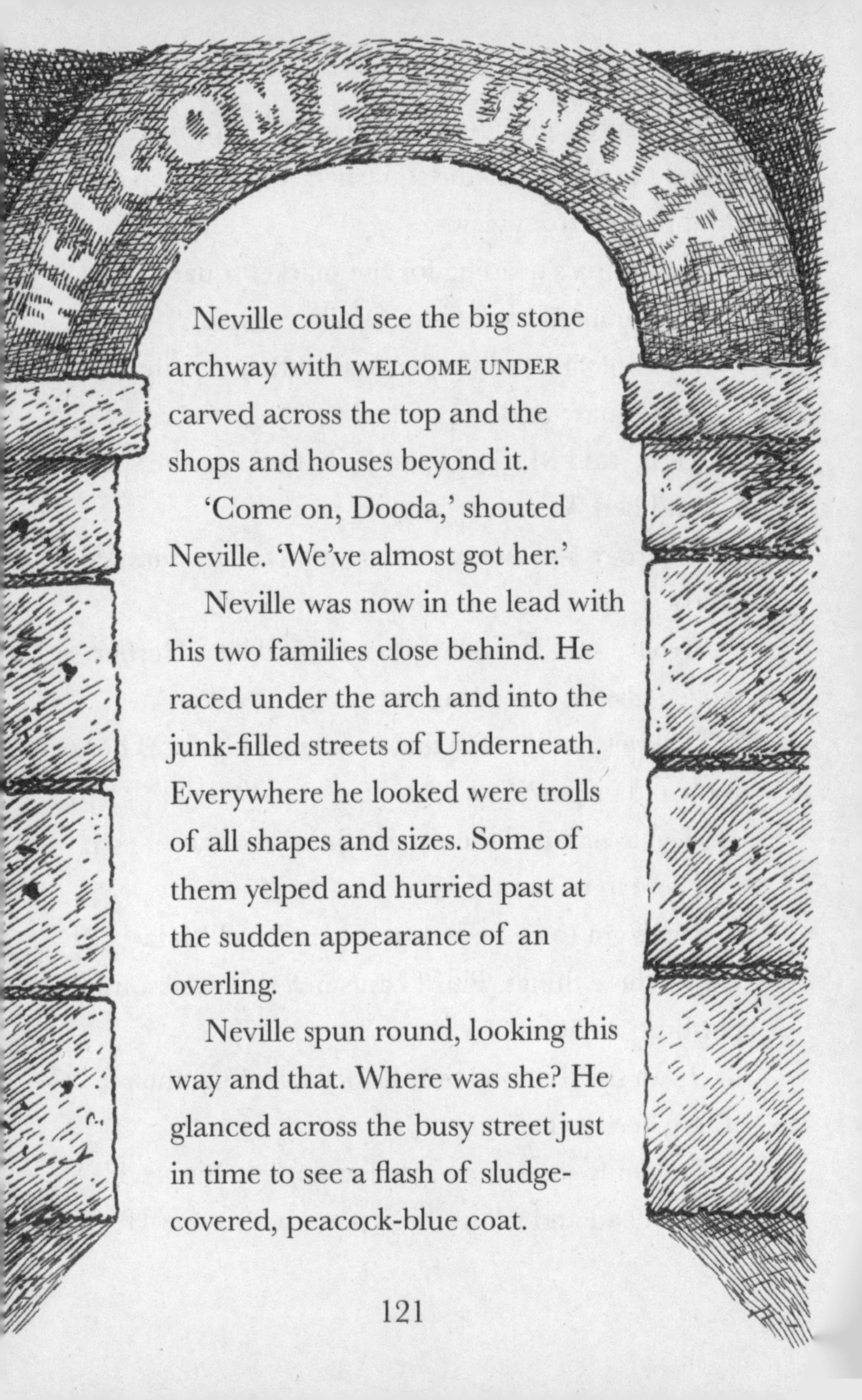

Neville could see the big stone archway with WELCOME UNDER carved across the top and the shops and houses beyond it.

'Come on, Dooda,' shouted Neville. 'We've almost got her.'

Neville was now in the lead with his two families close behind. He raced under the arch and into the junk-filled streets of Underneath. Everywhere he looked were trolls of all shapes and sizes. Some of them yelped and hurried past at the sudden appearance of an overling.

Neville spun round, looking this way and that. Where was she? He glanced across the busy street just in time to see a flash of sludge-covered, peacock-blue coat.

There was his grandma up ahead. She sprinted round the corner of the squashed squirrel shop and disappeared from view.

'Grandma's heading for the market square,' Neville shouted back to his families. 'Quick!'

The Bulches and the Briskets huffed into the market square and stopped.

'Ugh,' said Marjorie, suddenly noticing the scene around her. 'Where are we?'

'There're s-so many . . . s-so many –' stammered Herbert.

'Trolls,' said Rubella with a wicked leer. Herbert looked like he was going to cry.

'There's no time for that now,' said Clod. 'Where is the old griper?'

Neville scanned the square. Jaundice was nowhere to be seen.

'She's got to be here somewhere,' said Malaria. 'I knows these things. Plus I can smell that stinksome perfume she wears.'

'I can smell it too,' said Rubella, sniffing the air. 'But where is she?'

Suddenly something small and metal hit Neville on the head and fell to the ground with a *ting.* He bent down and picked it up. It was a small bolt with a tiny piece of peacock-blue thread caught on one of the corners.

Neville looked up. They were standing right below the ticker-dinger-thinger. He peered through the cogs and swinging pendulums of the enormous junk clock.

'I think I know – THERE SHE IS!' Neville pointed excitedly.

Jaundice was high above them, swinging from pendulum to pendulum inside the ticker-dinger-thinger.

'Well done, Nev,' Clod beamed. 'You've got eyes like a right blinker, you have.'

Herbert looked up and called out, 'Hold on, Mummy!'

'Right,' said Marjorie suddenly. 'How are we going to catch the weasel?'

'Marjorie!' gasped Herbert.

'I haven't been flushed down a toilet, dunked in sludge and paraded into a troll town just to let the old bat get away now.'

Marjorie put Napoleon down, rolled up her sleeves and gritted her teeth. Neville wasn't sure, but he thought he might actually have heard her growl.

'Let's get her!' shouted Rubella.

By now, other trolls were wandering over to see what all the commotion was about. No one had ever seen so many overlings all at once. They pushed and shoved to get a closer look. One even picked up a stick and prodded Herbert in the belly.

'Do you mind!' snapped Herbert.

'Quiet, Hergberg,' said Clod and raised his arm to the crowd. 'Fellow underlings . . . The Troll That Stole is back!' He pointed to where Jaundice was swinging high above. 'She's been hiding with the overlings and pretending to be one of them. We've got to put her away once and for all!'

A murmur rippled across the crowd.

'WALLOP THE OLD SKUNK!' screamed Marjorie.

The crowd of trolls all cheered.

'Lock her up!'

'Stop her!'

'Let's grab her!'

'AAAAARRRGGH!'

'Come on!' shouted Neville, feeling more brave than Captain Brilliant. He jumped into the air and caught hold of a low-swinging pendulum as it hurtled past. '*This way!*'

With that, hundreds of trolls ran to the base of the ticker-dinger-thinger and started to climb up through the mechanism with Neville, the Bulches and the Briskets in the lead.

The Troll That Stole

Jaundice ripped off a huge metal cog and threw it with all her troll-sized strength.

'RUBELLA!' Neville yelled. Rubella was hanging from a wooden beam, right in the path of the cog as it clanged down through the clock like a coin in one of those fancy moneyboxes at the supermarket. Just in time, Neville grabbed her wrist and yanked her safely out of the way.

'GET OFF!' she hissed.

'I just saved your life!'

'What d'you want? A medal or something? Pffffftttt!'

'GIVE UP, YOU SLUGS!' Jaundice bellowed, and continued to climb.

'She's gone all numb in the noggin,' said Clod as Malaria caught up with them. 'If she keeps climbing, she'll have no place left to go.'

Neville and his families were now high up inside the junk clock. So high, it made Neville feel dizzy and sick. What was he going to do? If he caught up with Jaundice, he couldn't fight her. By now, she had swelled to the same size as Rubella. His grandma would squash him like an ant.

CLANG-ANG-ANG-ANG! A clock hand careered past them on its way down to the market square below.

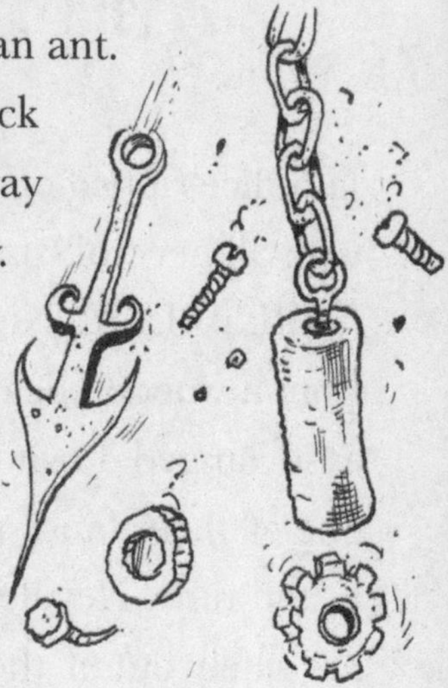

'She's getting scared,' said Malaria. 'Old Jaundice has got herself stuck like a toad in a toaster.'

'Come on!' shouted Rubella. 'Let's throw her off the top.'

'You can't do that,' said Clod. 'She'll leave an 'orrible mess.'

Neville looked up. They were right at the top of the ticker-dinger-thinger. Above, he could see Jaundice desperately scrabbling to find things to throw from a little ledge between hundreds of swinging weights and arms and pendulums.

'I'll flatten every last one of you!' she cackled. 'Just you watch.'

'Mummy,' came Herbert's voice from somewhere below. 'This isn't very nice.'

Then came the sound of Marjorie screaming again. Her bravery had run out when she'd realized how high up she was and now she clung to an old piece of lamp post with her eyes gripped shut and her mouth hanging open.

Another huge chunk of metal screamed past. Jaundice was practically tearing the clock to pieces. What could they do? Neville looked for something to grab or use. He just needed something to stop the crazy old troll from throwing any more clock parts.

That's when he noticed the huge whirring cog above Jaundice's head. It spun round, clicking noisily, and triggered hundreds of smaller cogs that made the pendulums swing to and fro.

'I've got an idea,' said Neville.

'Oh, jubbly,' said Clod. 'What's 'at then?'

'Take off your belt, Dooda.'

'Do what?' said Clod. 'I can't do that. Me trousers will fall off.'

'You'll just have to hold them up,' said Neville. 'I need the hooks.'

'Do what Nev says,' said Malaria. 'You know he's the brain-bulgiest one. Get that belt off, my brandyburp.'

Clod removed his belt with all the hooks for hanging fish and handed it to Neville. 'I hope you know what you're up to, Nev.'

'I hope so too,' said Neville. His belly started growling with nervousness. This was it. He swung the belt above his head as fast as he could.

'Get on with it, dungle dropping,' said Rubella as a big piece of wood bounced off her head.

'Shhhh, Nev's concentratin',' said Malaria.

'Good luck, Nev,' beamed Clod, giving Neville a friendly wink. 'You can do it.'

Neville spun the belt faster and faster above his head. He locked his eyes on the small platform between the pendulums and waited for a gap as they hurtled left and right, left and right.

He gritted his teeth, scrunched his toes and then,

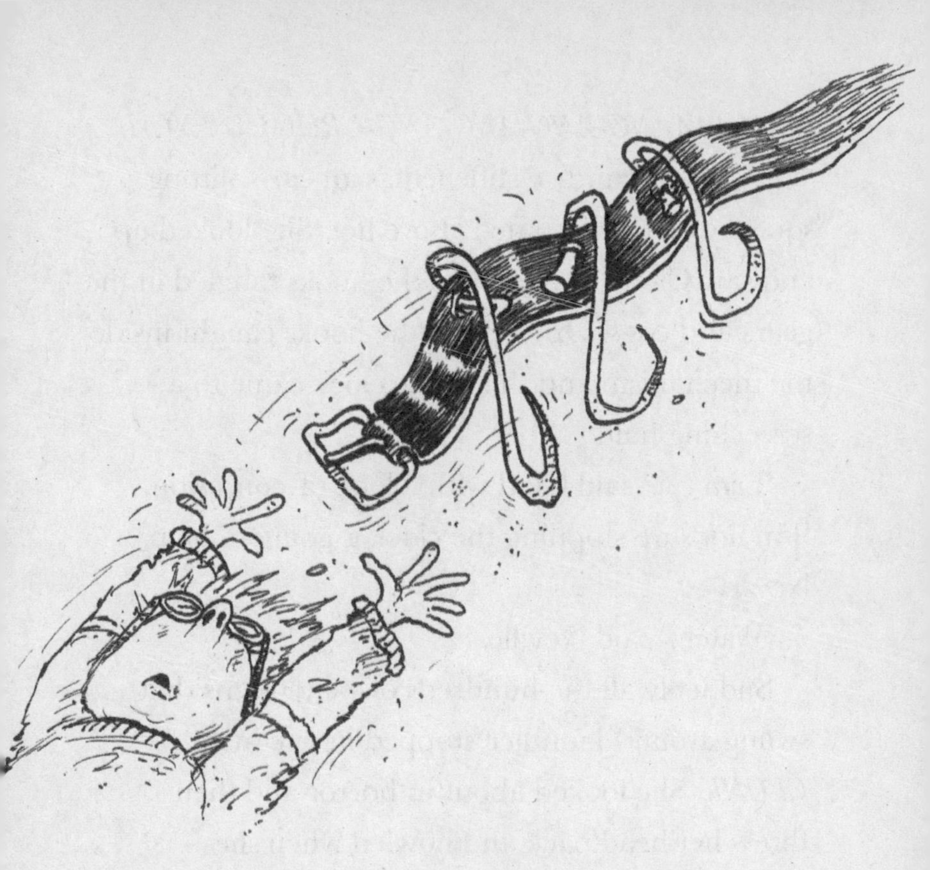

just when it looked like Neville was going to stand there swinging the belt all day, he let go of it.

Everything went silent as every troll on the clock held their breath and watched. The belt whizzed through the air and shot straight past Jaundice.

'HA!' she laughed. 'YOU MISSED, YOU USELESS LITTLE NOBODY!'

'I wasn't aiming for you,' Neville yelled back with a grin.

CLAAAANG-ANG-ANG-ANG-CRUUUUUNCH!

'Wha–?' Jaundice stiffened as an ear-splitting squeal of metal boomed above her. She looked up and saw Clod's belt with all the hooks tangled in the gears and cogs. One by one the hooks caught inside the mechanism and the whole clock came to a screeching halt.

'Erm . . .' said Clod with a look of confusion. 'I'm not sure stopping the clock is going to help, Nev.'

'Watch,' said Neville.

Suddenly all the hundreds of pendulums that swung around Jaundice stopped in one huge *CLUNK*. She looked about in horror and then threw her head back and howled when she realized what had happened.

'NOOOOOOOOOOOOOOOOOOO!!'

'Well, I'll be a winkle's wotzit,' said Malaria. 'He's only gone and done it.'

'You got her, Nev,' cheered Clod.

'I could have done that,' Rubella grunted. 'That was . . . rubbish!'

Neville smiled to himself and felt his cheeks going red. He felt as brave as . . . no . . . *braver* than

Captain Brilliant. The platform and all the frozen pendulums had formed a perfect and very impenetrable cage round Lady Jaundice.

The Troll That Stole was back in prison.

Too-Da-Loo

Herbert stood trembling and looked like he'd had his brains scrambled. Clod wandered over slowly and put a hand on his shoulder.

'Not to fret, Hergberg,' Clod said with a rosy smile. 'I found out my mooma was half a hinkapoot when I was a lumpling. It don't mean no nevermind.'

Herbert opened his mouth to speak, but nothing came out.

'It's OK, Dad,' said Neville. He was wearing a crown made from an old paint can that a happy troll had made for him at the top of the ticker-dinger-thinger. 'Grandma is where she belongs. And besides, we could always come and visit.'

'Fat chance,' grunted Marjorie. 'Now can we please go home?'

The Bulches and the Briskets were standing in

the pipe chamber, next to the Bulches' pipe.

'I suppose we should get back,' said Neville with a heavy heart. He liked being back in the Underneath. He didn't even mind the toadstool that had sprouted on the side of his neck. 'But what about the ticker-dinger-thinger? What will you do now that it's stopped?'

'Oh, don't you worry,' said Clod. 'Now we've got her, Jaundice'll be locked and lunked back up in proper jail. With a bit of elbow greasin' we'll have the ticker-dinger-thinger back up and running in no time.'

'Indeedy we will, Nev,' said Malaria. 'Don't you fret none.'

'It really was a squibbly old trolliday,' Clod whispered to Neville. 'I hope your dad's all right.'

Neville shrugged. 'Who knows,' he said. 'At least it put a little bit of excitement into their lives.'

'Oh, Nev, you are naughtsie,' laughed Malaria. 'I'm blunkin' proud of you, my lump.'

'What about me?' snuffed Rubella. 'I helped.'

'Yeah,' Neville mumbled sarcastically. 'Couldn't have done it without you.'

'You too, Belly,' said Malaria before Rubella

could thump him. 'I'm just glad my good looks have returned now that we're back where it's dark and dooky.' She planted a big sloppy kiss on Neville's head. 'Say too-da-loo, Pong.'

Pong jumped out of his mooma's arms and licked Neville's cheeks.

'See you soon, Nev,' she smiled. Then she ushered Marjorie and Herbert towards the pipe.

'Bye, foozleface,' said Rubella flatly. 'Don't even think about hugging me.'

Neville smiled and hugged Rubella's belly anyway. She grimaced and made throwing-up noises.

'Come along, Neville,' Herbert said. 'NOW!' Then without even saying goodbye to the Bulches, he turned and shot up the pipe.

'Wait for me,' Marjorie whimpered. She gripped Napoleon to her chest and vanished up the pipe with a slurpy, gurgling sound.

'Bye, Dooda,' said Neville, hugging Clod's knee.

'Next time you see the moon,' said Clod, 'say hello for me, will you?'

'Of course,' said Neville.

'That's m'lump. See you soon, hero.' Then Clod

kissed Neville's head. 'I'll make sure to pass a few rat patties through the bars for your granny from time to time.'

Neville sighed to himself and smiled. It was fun having a mum and dad, and a mooma and dooda.

He wriggled into the pipe and shot off into the darkness. Neville barely noticed the whooshing and twisting, he was so happy.

With a splash of toilet water, his bathroom came into view. He stepped on to the tiles among a mound of dislodged bricks and cement, and shook the drips out of his clothes.

'That was squibbly,' he mumbled to himself.

Neville opened the bathroom door to go off to bed and instantly had a broom, a mop, some rubber gloves and a bucket stuffed into his arms. Marjorie stood before him in the hallway with a face like thunder. Neville wasn't sure, but he thought he could almost see smoke coming out of her ears.

'NEVILLE BRISKET!' she screamed. 'GET TO WORK!'

'Ello, my pluglets. By now, I'm sure you're chatty-wagging left, right and under with all the trollish words you've learned. Here's a few more for you to practise . . .

Blinker	A person with very good eyesight
Boogle	To burst
Brainy-bonker	A very clever person
Bumfy	Calm, cosy and comfortable
Chattywag	A good ol' gossip
Chuffer	A very happy person
Dooky hole	The grimiest place in the Underneath
Exciterous	Exciting
Fun-poked	Teased
Funksome	Strange
Fuzzbonk	An ugly, ugly person

Gentlegeorge	A gentleman
Glump	A trudge or a long, slow walk
Glumper	A tiresome, moaning person
Grunch	To eat

Grunty-groaner	A worrier
Gundiskump	An enormous, greedy fish
Gurnip	A name for a very old person
Jiggish	Fun
Jubbly	Lovely
Moodsie	Grumpy

Nervish	Nervous
Nipster	A toddler
Nonkumbumps	Nonsense
Panty-bloomers	Overling underwear
Porklet	A young, chubby thing
Snizzling	Snoring
Squirmer	Coward
Trolliday	A troll holiday

Truccaneer	A troll pirate
Wonderbunk	Wonderful
Winky	Tiny

You'll laugh your panty-bloomers off with these little belly-bunglers . . .

Q. What is Lady Jaundice's favourite game?
A. Swallow the leader!

Q. Why did Malaria eat Marjorie's sofa?
A. Because she had a suite tooth!

Q. What do you get if you cross Rubella with a flea?

A. A lot of very worried dogs!

Q. Why did Grandma Joan take a bath?

A. So she could make a clean getaway!

Q. What do trolls eat for breakfast?

A. Dreaded wheat!

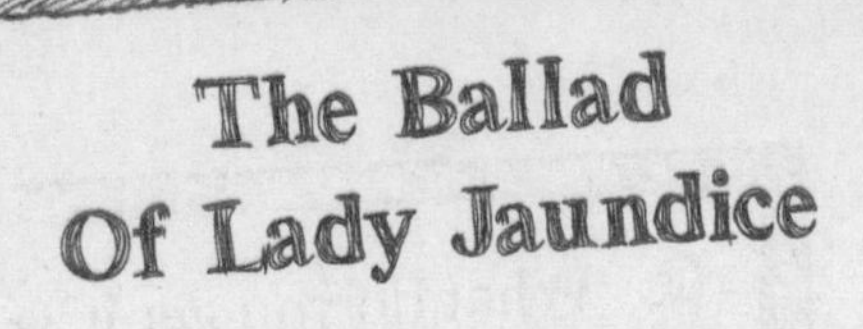

At the moment she was born, a cry went all
about.
'Lock the little rotter up and never let her
out!'
She'd a gonker for a mother and a blighter
for a dad.
It didn't take a brainy-bonk to see she would
be bad.
For even as a nipster she wore an evil sneer,
That nasty, thieving dungle of a trainee
truccaneer.

Marauder of the mud-beds and fungus fiend was she.
The Troll That Stole was destined to go down in
history.

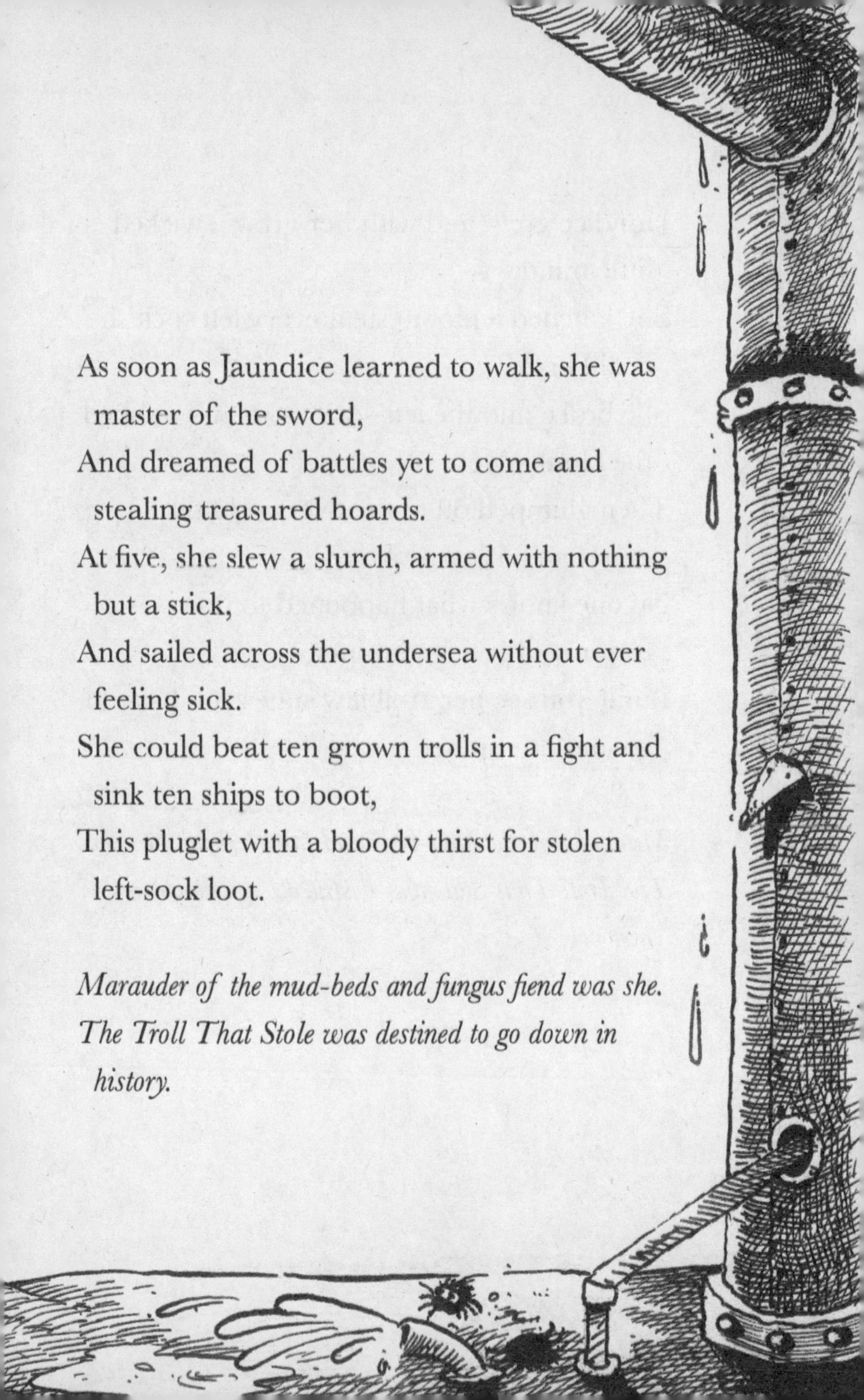

As soon as Jaundice learned to walk, she was master of the sword,
And dreamed of battles yet to come and stealing treasured hoards.
At five, she slew a slurch, armed with nothing but a stick,
And sailed across the undersea without ever feeling sick.
She could beat ten grown trolls in a fight and sink ten ships to boot,
This pluglet with a bloody thirst for stolen left-sock loot.

Marauder of the mud-beds and fungus fiend was she.
The Troll That Stole was destined to go down in history.

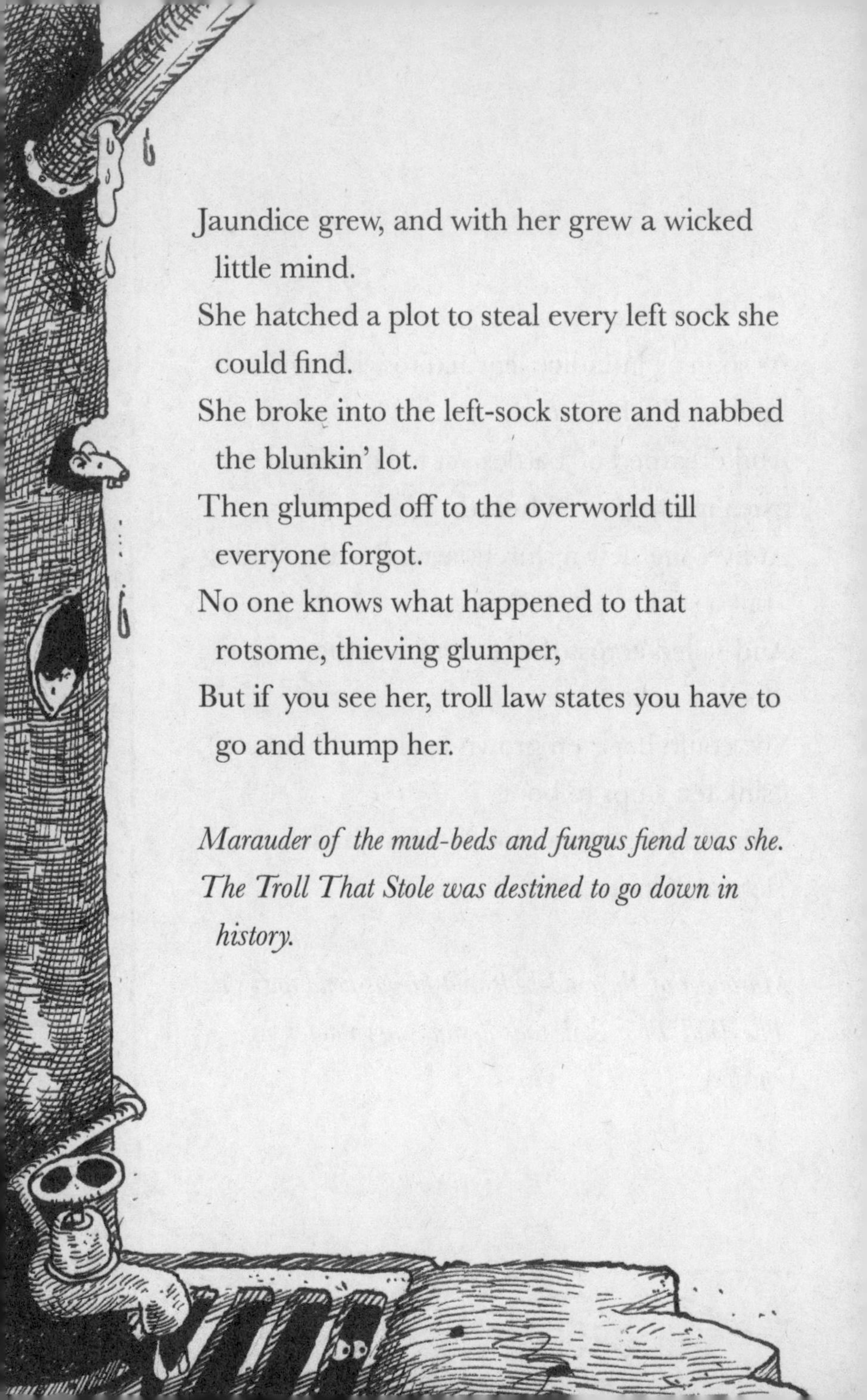

Jaundice grew, and with her grew a wicked
little mind.
She hatched a plot to steal every left sock she
could find.
She broke into the left-sock store and nabbed
the blunkin' lot.
Then glumped off to the overworld till
everyone forgot.
No one knows what happened to that
rotsome, thieving glumper,
But if you see her, troll law states you have to
go and thump her.

Marauder of the mud-beds and fungus fiend was she.
The Troll That Stole was destined to go down in
history.

Turn over to read about Neville's funksome first night in the Underneath . . .

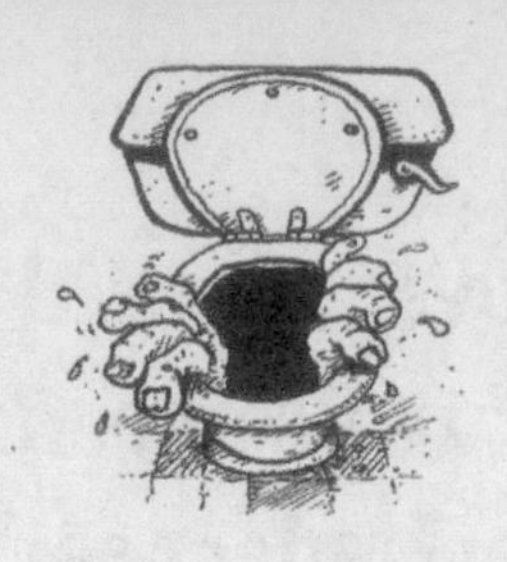

The Wrong Pong

With a great big whoosh, Neville found himself falling at a ferocious speed through a foul-smelling, rusty pipe. The water around him splooshed and churned as he was spun down into the darkness.

A hefty arm suddenly wrapped itself round Neville's waist. He squirmed but the arm held tight.

'Up we go,' came a voice behind Neville. He heard the sound of a chain being grabbed and he was swung up out of the disgusting water and into the air.

Neville landed on his belly with a BUMP.

'Oooooof!'

He clambered to his feet, coughing and spluttering out the rotten taste of toilet before he was sick. What was going on? Neville started to cry. He couldn't see anything in the gloom. Mum was always telling him there were no such things as toilet monsters and now one had got him.

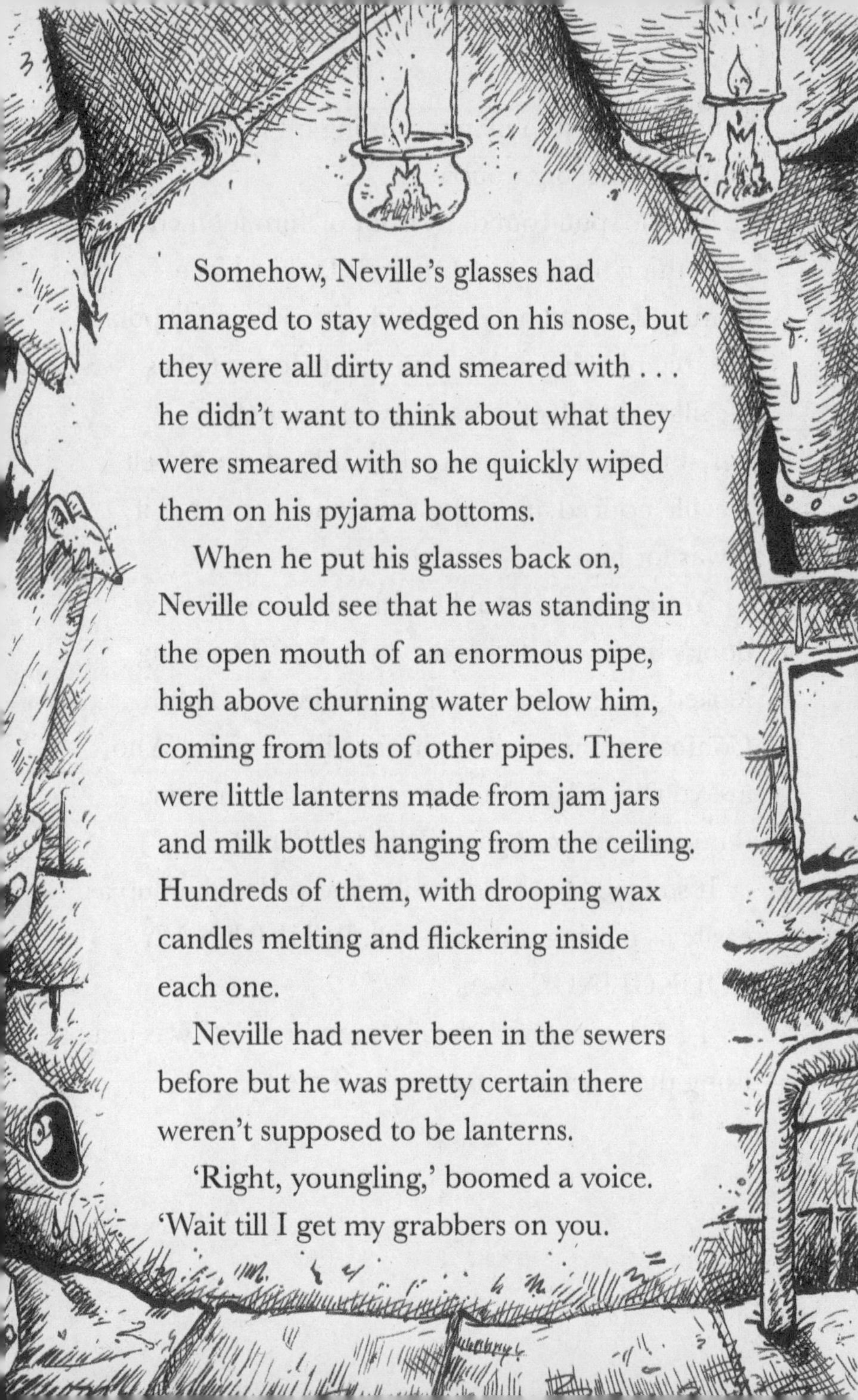

Somehow, Neville's glasses had managed to stay wedged on his nose, but they were all dirty and smeared with . . . he didn't want to think about what they were smeared with so he quickly wiped them on his pyjama bottoms.

When he put his glasses back on, Neville could see that he was standing in the open mouth of an enormous pipe, high above churning water below him, coming from lots of other pipes. There were little lanterns made from jam jars and milk bottles hanging from the ceiling. Hundreds of them, with drooping wax candles melting and flickering inside each one.

Neville had never been in the sewers before but he was pretty certain there weren't supposed to be lanterns.

'Right, youngling,' boomed a voice. 'Wait till I get my grabbers on you.

What were you thinking, running off like that? You're in big, big trouble.'

Neville spun round. In front of him loomed something from a nightmare. It looked like a human that had been crossed with a knobbly potato or a big old ginger root and was twice as tall as Neville's dad. It was fussing with a batch of ugly-looking fish hanging from a hook on its belt. Neville noticed an empty hook and wondered if it was for him.

'Your mooma would knock you through next-door's back wall if she knew you . . .' The thing looked up and saw Neville in the lantern light. Confusion spread across its face like a rash. 'Who are you?' it asked. Neville couldn't say anything. 'You ain't my youngling! Where's Pong?'

It stormed towards Neville and picked him up as easily as picking up a rag-doll. 'WHERE'S MY YOUNGLING?'

'I-I-I don't know,' Neville stammered. 'I was just using the toilet and you grabbed me.'

Simply subscribe here to become a member

puffinpost.co.uk

and wait for your copy to decorate your doorstep.

(WARNING – reading *Puffin Post* may make you late for school.)

It all started with a Scarecrow.

Puffin is seventy years old.

Sounds ancient, doesn't it? But Puffin has never been so lively. We're always on the lookout for the next big idea, which is how it began all those years ago.

Penguin Books was a big idea from the mind of a man called Allen Lane, who in 1935 invented the quality paperback and changed the world. **And from great Penguins, great Puffins grew, changing the face of children's books forever.**

The first four Puffin Picture Books were hatched in 1940 and the first Puffin story book featured a man with broomstick arms called Worzel Gummidge. In 1967 Kaye Webb, Puffin Editor, started the Puffin Club, promising to **'make children into readers'.** She kept that promise and over 200,000 children became devoted Puffineers through their quarterly instalments of *Puffin Post*, which is now back for a new generation.

Many years from now, we hope you'll look back and remember Puffin with a smile. **No matter what your age or what you're into, there's a Puffin for everyone.** The possibilities are endless, but one thing is for sure: whether it's a picture book or a paperback, a sticker book or a hardback, **if it's got that little Puffin on it – it's bound to be good.**